Mixed Grill by William Pett Ridge

William Pett Ridge was born at Chartham, near Canterbury, Kent on 22nd April 1859.

His family's resources were certainly limited. His father was a railway porter, and his son, after schooling in Marden, Kent became a clerk in a railway clearing-house. The hours were long and arduous, but self-improvement was his goal. After working from nine until seven o'clock he attended evening classes at Birkbeck Literary and Scientific Institute and then he would write.

From 1891 his humourous sketches were published in the St James's Gazette, the Idler, Windsor Magazine and other literary periodicals of the day. He was heavily influenced by Dickens and critics thought he might be his successor.

Pett Ridge published his first novel in 1895, A Clever Wife. By his fifth novel, Mord Em'ly, three years later, his success was obvious. His writing was written from the perspective of those born with no privilege and relied on talent to find humour and sympathy in his portrayal of working class life.

Today Pett Ridge and other East End novelists including Arthur Nevinson, Arthur Morrison & Edwin Pugh are grouped together as the Cockney Novelists.

With his success Pett Ridge gave generously of both time and money to charity. In 1907 he founded the Babies Home at Hoxton, one of several children's organisations

His circle considered Pett Ridge to be one of life's natural bachelors. In 1909 they were rather surprised therefore when he married Olga Hentschel.

As the 1920's arrived Pett Ridge added to his popularity with the movies. Four of his books were adapted into films.

Pett Ridge now found the peak of his fame had passed. He still managed to produce a book a year but was falling out of fashion and favour with the reading public. His canon runs to over sixty novels and short-story collections as well as many pieces for magazines and periodicals.

William Pett Ridge died, on 29th September 1930, at his home, Ampthill, Willow Grove, Chislehurst, at the age of 71.

Index of Contents

I

THIRD PERSON SINGULAR

I met him when I was in town at a party, where he and I were about the only grown-ups; he took a good deal of trouble over the youngsters, doing conjuring tricks to amuse them, and singing songs at the piano-forte that made them laugh. Later in the evening, when some of the kids had been fetched, he and I became friendly, and we had a most interesting chat. He agreed with my views regarding the Australian team of the previous summer; he was in full sympathy concerning the difficulty of making one pair of white gloves do for two evenings. I asked for his name and address.

"Don't think I have a card to spare, old chap," he said, in his easy way. "Daresay we shall meet again."

"I'd awfully like to make sure of it," I said. "My mother may want you to run down to our place."

"That's a different matter. Here's a pencil; write it on something. Or allow me. I'm coming back here at ten," he went on. "You won't be gone before that, I hope?"

"I must!' I replied. "My governess will call at half-past nine to take me home."

"What an existence we men about town do live, to be sure. Always hurrying from one place to another."

"If my mother writes to you, Mr. Cartwright," I said, offering my hand, "you won't fail to come along."

My mater is peculiar; she has a fixed and permanent idea that any suggestion coming from me must necessarily be over-ruled and treated as of no serious importance; I fancy this comes from the feeling, often expressed by her, that she has to be both father and mother. It is rather a lonely life for her, with only my governess and the servants for company. I have heard the maids saying more than once to each other that they wondered mistress did not marry again. "She could well afford to," remarked cook.

I do think I showed cleverness and tact something very like high diplomacy. I reminded my mother of the parties I had attended, and said I felt glad there was no necessity for us to have our house turned upside down and to give an evening in return. At lunch time I referred to the matter again. Later I said good-night to her, and once more made similar allusion to the subject.

Cards of invitation went out the next day, and my governess started on the preparation of a charade. My governess is not, if I may say so, possessed of incredible cleverness, and after writing out the charade and starting rehearsals, she found she had forgotten the word, and as no one could guess it, and she appeared unable to think of another, it became evident that we could not rely upon this as a source of entertainment. It was then I announced to my mother that I had already sent a note to a friend of mine, a man whose equal for entertaining a party was rarely encountered, and that I expected a reply from him in the course of a post or two. She blamed me for taking the step without asking permission, and praised me for coming to the rescue with such an excellent idea.

"Did you say Cartwright Mr. Cartwright, dear?"

"Yes, mother. Do you know him?"

"I don't think I have met the name."

When Mr. Cartwright's postcard arrived, and the maid put it by the side of my plate, my mother, glancing down the table before opening her own letters, asked quickly from whom it had come, and when I told her she contradicted me, quoting, rather excitedly, the usual Biblical and historical cases where severe punishment had been given for the telling of lies, or commendation awarded for the statement of exact truth. I ventured to repeat the information, and passed the card to her as a document in support; she looked at it, cried a little, and asked me to forgive her for being so cross. I begged her not to mention it.

"Just for the moment," she explained, "it took me back about twelve years."

"Before my time, mother?"

"Yes. You were not thought of then. Does your friend sign himself Cartwright?"

"My dear mother, how else could he sign himself?"

"Send him another line, and say that your mother is looking forward to the pleasure of making his acquaintance."

"You must tell me how to spell some of the words," I said.

The carriage was to meet some of the guests who came from London, and I went down to the station myself and arranged with one of the cabmen there, so that Mr. Cartwright should be brought up alone and without being crowded by the children. My mother said I could ask him to stay the night, and ordered a room at the hotel; but he wrote to say he had another engagement in town, and he desired to catch the seven fifty-four back. I remarked that this showed how popular he was in society; my mother gave a word approving business-like habits. It seemed exactly like Mr. Cartwright that he should arrive in the cab at the precise hour arranged.

"Had a good journey?" I cried, running to him in the hall as he was getting out of his thick overcoat. "I was afraid, somehow, that you'd back out of it at the last moment."

"Never disappoint the public," he replied cheerfully. "Sometimes I disappoint myself, but that is another matter."

I asked what he had in his large bag.

"Brought down a figure; thought perhaps a little ventriloquism would be a novelty."

"Anything you do will be sure to be appreciated. I've been thinking ever since I met you of the perfectly splendid way you entertained at that party."

"Good man!"

"And I do feel it's most awfully kind of you to come all this distance just to oblige me. Let's go upstairs, shall we, Mr. Cartwright? I'll take you to the room that used to be called the nursery."

He got rid of his overcoat there, and, asking me for a pair of scissors, went carefully with them around the edge of his shirt cuffs. I inquired whether he had been going out to many parties since I last saw him: he replied that he had no right to complain; there were plenty of exceedingly clever people about and he could only regard himself as cleverish. I exhibited the soldiers that mother had given me for my birthday. He took the blue men, I took the red, and he was Napoleon and I Wellington. We sat upon the floor, and he was so very good as to show me exactly what happened at the battle of Waterloo, an incident of peculiar interest to me, because it occurred on one of the few dates I am able to retain in my memory.

"But, Mr. Cartwright, how is it you know so much about this? ' He was moving some dominoes up from the right to represent the approach of Blucher and the German troops.

"Used to be a soldier man,' he replied. "Why ever didn't you stay in the army, and become a Field Marshal?"

"By Jove!" he cried, "that would have been a rattling good idea. Wonder I didn't think of it at the time."

"Is it too late now?"

"Surely not," he answered promptly, "for such an exceptionally fortunate person as I am. Anyway, so far as 1815 is concerned, Blucher, you see, had Grouchy to compete with this double-six is Grouchy, with thirty-five thousand men but Blucher outmarched him, came up, and—" He swept the rest of his blue men down with a wave of the hand, and hummed "Rule, Britannia."

I expressed a wish that he had selected the reds, so that he might have won; but he remarked in a change of mood that anything like success in any game would, by reason of its novelty, have given him serious alarm. I asked how the time was going.

"Lent my watch to a relative," he mentioned. "A rather distant relative; but I see a good deal of him, from the waist upwards."

And he went to the mantelpiece to inspect the clock.

"Little man," in a sharp voice, "who is this?"

"That? Oh, that's dear mother."

He looked at it closely, whistled a tune softly.

"I shall have to catch an earlier train," he announced suddenly. "I'm sorry. You make my apologies to every one, and say the muddle was entirely mine."

"But you can't, Mr. Cartwright. There's nothing before the six minutes to eight."

My governess came in, and he replaced the frame quickly. My governess has sometimes complained that the house is lacking in male society; she took advantage of this opportunity to talk with great vivacity, and, in tones very different from those she uses in addressing me, inquired with affectation concerning the theatres in town, and entertainments generally. Fearing she would try Mr. Cartwright's patience, as she has often tried mine, I endeavoured to detach her; but the task proved one beyond my abilities, and she went on to submit, with deference, that what was required was an increase of merriment in life, a view that, coming from her, amazed me into silence. Mr. Cartwright answered that in his opinion life was full of rollicking fun, completely furnished with joy. "What a gift," cried my governess, "to be able always to see the cheerful side! It means, of course, that you have been singularly free from anything like disaster. Tell me, now, what is the nearest to a sad experience that you ever had?"

"I expect we ought to be getting downstairs," he remarked.

In the hall I introduced Mr. Cartwright, with pride, to my mother.

"Charmed to meet you," she said, offering her hand. My mother can be very pleasant, and if, at the moment, she gave signs of agitation, it was not to be wondered at; I myself felt nervous. "My boy tells me that you are going to be so very kind—" She appeared unable to go on with the sentence.

"I was glad," he said, "to find he had not forgotten me. It isn't everybody who has a good memory."

"It isn't everybody who cares to possess one," she said, with some spirit. "I have heard of cases where men forget their real names."

"I have heard of cases," he remarked, "where women have been in a great hurry to change theirs."

It struck me they were not hitting it off, as one might say, and I took his hand and led him into the drawing-room, where the children were having refreshment between the dances. He made himself at home with them at once, danced a quadrille with the smallest girl, consulted with my governess about the playing of some accompaniments, and amused her by a remark which he made. A man who could make my governess laugh was a man capable of anything. Going to the end of the room, he took a figure of a boy in a Tarn o' Shanter cap out of his bag, and, setting it upon his knee, started absolutely the best entertainment I have seen in the whole course of my existence. We all rested on the floor; my mother stood near the doorway, but I was too much interested in Mr. Cartwright's performance to pay attention to her. When I did look around once, to get her to join in the applause, I found she was looking hard at my friend, trying, I suppose, to find out how he did it. He began to sing, with the figure making absurd interruptions that sent us all into fits of laughter; my mother, still serious, took a chair. Mr. Cartwright had a good voice; I don't know whether you would call it a baritone or a tenor, but it was so pleasant to listen to that I half agreed with a sensible girl sitting just in front of me, who said she wished the figure would cease interfering.

'Lor" bless my soul," said the figure, "thought you'd never get that note, Mr. Cartwright. Only just managed it." And, in a confidential way, "Aren't you a rotten singer, though? Don't you think so, strictly between ourselves? Have you ever tried selling coke? That would be about your mark, you know!"

We clapped hands and stamped feet when he finished, and even the girls declared they would rather hear something more from him than go on with the dances. He looked at his watch, and I called out to him that he was all right for his train; he had a quarter of an hour to spare. He came back to the pianoforte. There he touched the keys, making a selection in his mind.

"No, no! I cried my mother, as the prelude to a song began. "Please, not that one!"

He changed the air at once, and went off into an Irish song. You know the kind of tune one that makes you keep on the move all the time you are listening. About a ball given by Mrs. O' Flaherty, where the fiddler, once started, declined to stop, and the couples kept on with the hop, hop, hop, so that the dance lasted for I forget how long three weeks, I think. The couples gradually became tired, the tune went slower and slower.

"Mr. Cartwright," cried my governess, in her high voice, "you ought to be a professional."

"I am a professional," he replied.

I rushed like mad out into the hall. I wanted to get the opportunity of thinking as hard and as swiftly as possible. There was no time to lose; the station cab stood outside the door, waiting for him. I went up, three stairs at a time, and opened the door of my room; it had been used as a temporary cloak-room, and jackets and hats were littered all over the place. As I threw these about everything had been moved by the servants with some idea of making elaborate preparations it struck me it was not unlike a nightmare; one of those nightmares where you are in a most terrific hurry, and everything slips away and eludes you. I could have cried with annoyance at the thought that Mr. Cartwright was now preparing to leave, asking for me, perhaps, and certainly wondering when and how he was to receive his fee for making the special visit from town. In my excitement I took the pillow and threw it into the air; underneath I found my money-box, and some other articles which had been shifted from the dressing-table. I seized one of my dumb-bells, smashed the box, counted out the money with trembling fingers.

"Four and three," I said to myself. "I shall give him four shillings, and tell him I'll send the rest on."

I slid down two flights. As I neared the landing above the hall I could hear that music had started afresh and dancing had recommenced. I was engaged to a rather sensible girl already referred to for the polka, and she would be looking out for me; but for the moment I was too full of troubles of my own to consider those of other people. The front door was open, and my mother was waving her hand.

"Mr. Cartwright!" I called out, running past her. "Mr. Cartwright! Oh, do let me speak to you for a minute."

"Can't stop, old boy," he said from the cab. He seemed rather quiet.

"But I must speak to you. Mother, may I go down to the station with him? Oh, you are a good sort," as she nodded her consent. I jumped in, and the cab started.

I felt so thankful when I saw in his hand an envelope with some pieces of gold, and I felt proud of her. I might have guessed mother would know how to do the right thing.

"Little man!" He was looking at a slip of paper with some pencilled words which the envelope also contained. "Do you ever take advice, I wonder!"

"Do you, Mr. Cartwright?"

"I find it easier to give. People have been filling me up with it ever since I was about your age, and some of it has been good, but I have always done exactly as I pleased."

"I suppose that's the best plan."

"No!" he replied. "It has some advantages, but not many."

"But aren't you?" I scarcely knew how to phrase it "aren't you exactly what you want to be, Mr. Cartwright? You're so good-humoured and jolly."

He gave a gasp and looked at the window.

"I don't lose my temper now," he said. "I used to, and the last time I lost with it everything that was worth having. Here's the advice I want to give you. Forget me, but try to remember this. Quarrel, if you must quarrel, with the people who don't matter. Never quarrel with your friends. I had fierce words once with the best friend a man ever had."

"What was his name?"

"It has taken her twelve years to forgive me, and in that time I've gone to pieces. All just for the luxury of five minutes of wild talk. Here's the station; my wife will be waiting for me at the other end, to take the money I've earned." He laughed in a peculiar way. "Goodbye, old chap. Not too big for this, are you?" He placed his hands on either side of my face. "I wish oh, I wish you were my boy!"

My mother asked me, when I got back and told her, to show her exactly where he had kissed me, and she pressed her lips for some moments to the place on my forehead. Then we went in and brightened up the party.

II

A BENEVOLENT CHARACTER

A youth came into the small tobacconist's and inquired, across the counter, whether there happened to be in the neighbourhood a branch establishment of a well-known firm (mentioned by name) dealing in similar goods and guaranteeing to save the consumer thirty-three per cent. He required the information, it appeared, because he contemplated buying a packet of cigarettes.

No, said the proprietor (after he finished his speech and the youth had gone), not quite the limit. Near to the edge, I admit; but remembering my friend, Mr. Ardwick, I can't say it's what you'd call the highest possible. It was a privilege to know Ardwick; he was, without any doubt whatsoever, a masterpiece. I've give up all hopes of ever finding his equal.

He was a customer here at the time Mrs. Ingram had the shop and when I say customer, of course I don't mean that he ever handed over a single halfpenny. Mrs. Ingram had only been a widow for about a twelve-month, and naturally enough she liked gentlemen's society; and Ardwick, after he got his compensation out of the County Council that, by the by, was one of his triumphs he had nothing else to do, and he became very much attached to that chair what you're sitting on now. He'd call in to have a look at the morning paper, and read it through from start to finish; later in the day he'd call to see the evening paper, and keep tight hold of it till he'd come to the name of the printers at the foot of the last page. Between whiles he'd pretend to make himself handy at dusting the counter, and help himself to a pipe of tobacco, out of the shag-jar. It was a pretty sight to see old Ardwick, before he left of an evening, talk, as he filled a pocket with matches out of the stand, about the way the rich robbed the poor.

Having caught sight of Mrs. Ingram's pass-book that she was sending to the bank he offered to post it, and walked all the way to Lombard Street and stuck to the twopence Ardwick makes up his mind to take the somewhat desperate step of proposing to Mrs. I.

"Very kind of you," she says, "but I fancy, Mr. Ardwick, you're a shade too stingy to run in double harness with me. Poor Ingram," she says, "was always free-handed with his money, and if I should ever get married again it will have to be to some one of a similar disposition. But thank you all the same," she says, "for asking!"

Ardwick ran across his friend Kimball in Downham Road that evening and lent him a match, and said Kimball was the very party he wanted to meet. They had a long, confidential sort of talk together outside the fire-station, and they came to such high words that a uniformed man, who was talking to one of his girls, threatened to turn the hose on them. The two strolled down Kingsland Road in a cooler frame of mind, and when they said "Good-night" at the canal bridge Kimball promised to do the best for Mr. Ardwick that lay in his power. Kimball explained that he was not going to do it out of friendship, but mainly because his wife had recently docked his allowance, and, in consequence, he felt a grudge against the sex in general.

"I promise you," said Mr. Ardwick, still shaking his hand, "that you won't lose over the transaction."

"Knowing you as I do," remarked Kimball, "I quite recognise that it'll take a bit of doing to make anything out of it."

Mr. Ardwick was in the shop, here, the following afternoon. Mrs. Ingram felt surprised to see him at that hour, and she locks up the till pretty smartly and moves the box of World-Famed Twopenny Cheroots.

"Something you said, Mrs. Ingram," he began, "has been worryin' of me, and I've called round to talk it over. You seem to have got the impression in your mind that I'm, if anything, a trifle close with my money. I should like to convince you, ma'am, that you are doing me an injustice, and to prove it I'm going to adopt a very simple plan."

"Have you brought back that watch of mine I gave you to get mended?"

"One topic at a time," urged Mr. Ardwick. "My idea of benevolence is something wider and broader than that of most people." He glanced at the clock. ' What I propose to do is this. To the first customer what enters this shop after half-past three I shall present the sum of five pound."

"Five what?"

"Five quid," he said, in a resolute sort of manner. "The first one, mind you, after half-past three. It wants two minutes to the half-hour now. All you've got to do, ma'am, is to stand where you are, and to judge whether I'm a man of a generous disposition or whether I'm the opposite."

As the clock turned the half-hour an old woman came in and put down four farthings for snuff; when she had gone Mr. Ardwick mentioned that he knew for a fact that the clock was a trifle fast. An elderly gentleman in workhouse clothes came for a screw of tobacco; Mr. Ardwick pointed out to Mrs. Ingram that he never proposed to extend his offer to those supported by the State. Kimball arrived at twenty-five minutes to, and Mr. Ardwick glared at him privately for not keeping the appointment. Kimball bought a box of wooden matches, and was leaving the shop when Mr. Ardwick called him.

"My man," he said, "your face and your general appearance suggest you are not one of those who are termed favourites of fortune. Tell me, now, have you ever been the recipient, so to speak, of a stroke of luck?"

"Not to my knowledge, sir," said Kimball, answering very respectfully.

"Never had a windfall of any kind? No sudden descent of manna from above? Very well, then." Mr. Ardwick took out his cheque-book and asked Mrs. I. for pen and ink. "Be so kind as to give me your full name, and it will be my pleasure to hand you over a handsome gift. I hope you will lay out the sum to the best advantage, and I trust it may prove a turning-point, a junction as it were, in your life!

Mr. Ardwick was talking across the counter to Mrs. Ingram about the pleasures of exercising charity, and the duty of those who possessed riches towards them who had none, when a most horrible idea seemed to occur to him, and he darted out of the shop like a streak of lightning. In Kingsland Road he just caught a motor-omnibus that was going towards the City, and on the way through Shoreditch he complained, whilst he mopped his forehead, because the conductor did not make the bus go quicker. Near Cornhill there was a block of traffic, and he slipped down and ran for his life. As he came near the bank he caught sight of Kimball descending the steps. Mr. Ardwick threw himself, exhausted, across a dustbin on the edge of the pavement, and burst into tears.

He mentioned to me afterwards that it was not so much the loss of the money that affected him as the knowledge that a fellow-man had broke his word. That was what upset Mr. Ardwick. He tried to explain all this at the time to a City constable.

"You get away home," advised the City constable, "and try to sleep it off. That's your best plan. Unless you want me to take you down to Cloak Lane for the night."

Mr. Ardwick felt very much hurt at this insinuation on his character, because, partly on account of his principles and partly because he hated giving money away, he was strict teetotal; but the remark furnished him with an idea, and he acted on it without a moment's delay. He returned to Dalston Junction, and there, by great good luck, he found Kimball Kimball smoking a big cigar and trying to persuade a railway-porter to accept one.

Mr. Ardwick went up to him and took the cigar.

"I congratulate you 'eartily," he said, slapping Kimball on the shoulder in a jolly sort of way. "There isn't many that could brag of having done Samuel Ardwick in the eye, but I always admit it when I come across my superior. There's only one favour I want you to grant."

"You gave me the cheque, and I've got a perfect right to it. What we may have agreed upon beforehand has nothing whatever to do with the matter."

"All I ask you to do," went on Mr. Ardwick, "is to allow me to celebrate the occasion by inviting you to have a little snack at a restaurant close by. A meal, I mean. A proper dinner. Food, and a bottle of something with it."

"This don't sound like you," remarked Kimball.

"I shan't make the offer twice," warned Mr. Ardwick.

Kimball strolled along with him rather reluctantly and somewhat suspiciously up Stoke Newington Road. Mr. Ardwick stopped outside an Italian eating-place, had a good look at the prices of everything in a brass frame near the doorway, gave a deep sigh, and led the way in.

It was here that, in my opinion, Mr. A. made a blunder; he admitted himself to me later that he was not acquainted with the quality of the wine or the capacity of his friend Kimball. The foreign waiter, being told confidentially that price was an object, recommended a quarter-bottle of what he called Vin Ordinaire at sevenpence. It was only when Kimball was starting on the fourth of these that Mr. Ardwick discovered he could have sent out for a full bottle at the cost of one-and-nine. He himself took no food and no beverage of any description, but just sat back, smoking the cigar, totting up the expenses, and keeping a watchful eye on his guest.

"Is it a fruity wine?" asked Mr. Ardwick, when the last quarter-bottle was opened.

Kimball lifted up his glass.

"I shouldn't like to say there was much of that about it," he answered. "As a matter of fact, it doesn't taste of anything."

"But surely it goes to your head!"

"It goes to my head," agreed Kimball, "because I put it there; but it don't seem to have any effect on the brain. Sheer waste of my time, so far as I can gather."

"Look here!" said Mr. Ardwick, with a determined effort. "I want to have a quiet talk with you. I've stood this very excellent meal, and it's only right you should do something for me in return."

"Anything within reason."

"I'm not the man to ask you to do anything else. You've had your little joke at my expense and now my suggestion is that you hand across the five pounds, and we'll both have a good laugh over the transaction. I admit you played your part uncommonly well. You ran it rather close, and if you'd been a minute or so later, my lad, you'd have found the bank closed, and then I could have stopped payment."

"I got there," said Kimball, "at one minute past four, and the doors were shut!"

Mr. Ardwick settled up, and told Kimball exactly what he thought of him.

"Imposing on generosity," he said heatedly "that's your game!"

He went off home to write a letter to the bank, and to recognise that matters had, after all, turned out better than he might have expected. In the evening he made his usual call here, dressed up special, and evidently anxious to find out what sort of an effect his display of benevolence had made on Mrs. I.

"I can't help seeing," she said confidentially, taking the evening paper from another customer and handing it to Mr. Ardwick, "that I've, all along, done you an injustice. I liked your conversation, and I had no fault to find with your general behaviour; but somehow I had an idea that you rather over-did the economical."

"If I come across a really deserving case," remarked Mr. Ardwick modestly, "I'm prepared to give away my last penny. I don't say I scatter my money broadcast, but when I do give I give liberally and with both hands."

"I was telling the poor man," said Mrs. Ingram, "that he ought to feel very much indebted to you. You've stood him on his feet, so to speak, and, whatever it may lead to, he's only got you to thank."

"Don't make too much of a mere trifle."

"I advised him to put half of it away in the Post Office, and use the other half to rig himself out in a new suit and look respectable."

"Excuse me," interrupted Mr. Ardwick, rather anxiously, "but when did you say all this to him?"

"About a hour or so ago," she replied, "when he came in and asked me to change the cheque for him. Knowing all the circumstances, of course I didn't hesitate a single moment!"

I was doing a bit of debt-collecting at the time, said the proprietor of the tobacconist's shop, and that was how I became acquainted with Mrs. Ingram. She felt grateful over my success with what was undoubtedly a tough job, and one word led to another, and eventually I consented to propose to her. She'll be down directly. Wait and have a glance at her, and tell me if you think I acted wisely.

III

THE WONDERFUL START

Dazed by sudden introduction to a distinguished company, lie glanced eagerly and confusedly around in the hope of finding some one who would give him a smile of encouragement. The most distinguished of all, seated opposite to him, acknowledged his bow and gave the order that a chair should be offered, and this was accepted.

Conversation did not immediately turn upon his affairs, and the delay enabled him to lean back and compose his mind; presently, no doubt, the others would switch discussion to the subject which excused his presence in this magnificent building. It had a strong scent of newness, a suggestion of the slate pencils used for the purpose of calculations in his early youth, calculations which were so often incorrect that he remembered how frequently in setting down a total he instinctively rubbed it out, under the impression that whatever he had written must be wrong. He did not become really clever in the management of figures until his London life began in Tooley Street, and that seemed a good many centuries ago. What was it, '80 or '81? February of '80 it must have been; early part of February. Thirty-two years, that made him forty-six. He could remember the start quite clearly.

As he stepped out into a wooden shed that was called London Bridge Station, a matronly woman, to whom he gave assistance in finding an outside porter for her deal box, referred to him in a sentence of thanks as a smart little nipper, and this, an auspicious compliment, sent him to the barrier and out into Railway Approach with a good conceit of himself. In the telegraph-office he wrote on a form in a confident way, as though he had been used all his life to the dispatching of telegrams:

"Arrived safely. Good journey. Best love. BEN."

The clerk on the other side of the counter mentioned that it would stand a better chance of reaching its destination if the name and address of the recipient were filled in. This constituted something in the nature of a check, and in the adjoining parcels-office he endeavoured to apply a remedy by knocking peremptorily with twopence and demanding instant attention.

"In a hurry?" asked the porter, nettled. "Because, if so, you'd better wait till your hurry's over. Bad enough to be ordered about by grown-ups; I'm certainly not going to be dictated to by slips of boys. D'you hear?"

He urged that no harm had been intended.

"What you intend", said the porter, giving a snatch at the parcel, "and what you do are very different things. Now then, don't stand there all day gazing! What d' you want me to do with this? Boil it, or what"

The lad answered, with respect, that he desired it should be sent by Parcels Delivery to the Peckham address given on the label; the man inspected very carefully, in the evident hope of discovering some flaw or defect that would enable him to decline the commission. He had to be content with throwing it, with a whirl, through the air into a corner, snatching at the twopence and giving a curt order, "Now be off with you!" To the question concerning the whereabouts of Tooley Street, he replied that if the lad could fly, he might reach it in two seconds; assuming him not to be so exceptionally gifted, the time could be given as two minutes. "Thank you, very much indeed, sir, for all your kindness."

The man looked at him narrowly, to make certain that this remark was not intended as chaff, and, reassured on the point, came out of the office and walked with him down the slope, where they faced a large corner public-house plastered over with orange bills and, above, a banner which said imperatively "Vote for Clarke."

The porter explained the meaning of all this, and made two prophecies: first, that Dizzy would, as a result of the day's election, get a valentine; second, that Gladstone might be taken down a notch. Returning confidence for confidence, the lad told him this was his first day in London, and his father had urged him to be honest and straight. They parted on excellent terms.

The incident proved a faithful sample of the happenings of a wonderful day. On the first floor of the number which he held in his memory, the surroundings were so much at variance with early anticipations that he feared he had made some disastrous blunder, until Mr. Cruttwell, head of the firm, slapped him joyously on the shoulder, declaring he had arrived just in time to see the fun. The office was rather dark, because the windows were covered with election bills, but gas flared generously.

Everybody, from the head down to a clerk only slightly older than the new lad, smoked pipes or cigars; some appeared inclined to smoke both at once. The head, raising his voice that it might be heard above the clatter, introduced him, and six men came over at once, saying:

"How do, young Stansfield? Wish you could manage this for me."

And the lad found himself in the very thick of it, so to speak, without a moment's delay. Cheering from the street below came now and again, startling him and causing him to rush to the windows in the endeavour to ascertain the cause; gentlemen with silk hats at the backs of their heads ran up two stairs at a time to ask how things were going, or to give news of how things were going, bringing tasks or appealing for them, roaring suggestions or shouting advice, talking privately in one corner and illustrating their arguments by pencilling figures on the wall-paper.

At eleven o'clock Mr. Cruttwell took him out, and, carrying a square brown-paper parcel of cards, he made the acquaintance of Southwark under lively circumstances. Mr. Cruttwell did not seem to know exactly what to be doing, but his plan was never to cease doing something, and he constantly appealed to the lad.

"Come along, come along, come along! Don't lag, my boy, don't lag!" or, "Now then, slowcoach! Have you gone to sleep again? Keep your eyes open, for goodness sake, or we shall never win!"

A most unfair suggestion, for the only founded charge against young Stansfield was that he stared at everything going on; shops arrested him, sandwich men proved an effective bar to progress. In waiting outside a leather merchant's in St. Thomas's Street, a detachment of Borough youths of about his own age came up with a threatening air.

"Who you for?" they demanded menacingly.

"Find out!" he answered.

"Want your 'ead punched?"

"Yes!" he said.

Disinclined to comply with any request, they conferred amongst themselves.

"What's inside that parcel? What's inside that parcel? Going to tell us, or ain't you?"

He began to feel terrified, and looked around for assistance. The people who were standing by did not seem to have any prejudices on one side or the other, and he was preparing to use his left arm as a guard and the parcel in his right hand as a weapon, when Mr. Cruttwell fortunately reappeared. The lads scampered off.

"You're a plucky little chap," said Mr. Cruttwell, in good humour after his call and slightly more rosy in complexion. "Some country youngsters would have been afraid."

He proceeded to give a short political lecture as they strolled back under the arches to Tooley Street, asserting that the manner in which Stansfield had tackled the Borough lads should be the method adopted by Great Britain in dealing with Russia. Prince Gortschakoff might have counted himself clever, and was, no doubt, uncommonly wily, but we, too, had men just as ingenious, and this Gortschy had discovered, and others would discover to their cost. Mr. Cruttwell began to use oratorical gesture, and in one fine sweep of the arm sent the lad's bowler hat into the roadway, restoring it with an apology that made the owner feel on a manly level with the best.

"Don't go out to lunch," said Mr. Cruttwell, "in case anything crops up. Send for it, and charge it to the office!"

He awoke from these thoughts on hearing his name mentioned, but some one interrupted with a deferential, "Will you excuse me, my lord, if I—" Leaning back, he went on with the glance over his shoulder at the past.

Easy to recall everything that stood on the table at the lunch in Tooley Street, partly because he assisted at the preparation. Acting under orders, he spread the sheets of a financial paper and, still obeying commands, accepted a sovereign, and, scurrying across the roadway, went up the steps, bolted over the Approach (with a dreadful fear that he might be run down by twenty omnibuses), and at the hotel made cautious purchases, rejecting so many cold fowls that the lady who served him called the manageress, demanding whether, as she had always understood, the birds were to be sold in chronological order, or whether a customer was to be permitted to make selection. The manageress decided that both parties to the contest were right, and encouraged the young woman with the reminder that, in view of the pressure of the day, everything that could be called eatable would probably be sold out before closing time.

So young Stansfield, taking the parcels and dear life in his hands, made once more the risky journey across the Approach. This over, the skating horses on the descent of Tooley Street gave him no terrors.

"No, no, DO!" whispered one of the other juniors. "You mustn't sit down with them, my rustic friend. We shall have to wait on them, and what they leave we—"He gave the remainder of the sentence in pantomime.

"Then I hope they won't overdo it," remarked the lad. "I begin to feel puckish."

As lunch proceeded, the juniors cutting bread and filling glasses, men wearing favours who looked in at the doorway, crying, "Hallo, hallo! Feeding-time at the Zoo, eh?" were immediately invited to take knife and fork and help themselves, which they did with such enthusiasm that the juniors were near to the edge of tears, when Mr. Cruttwell stood up and said:

"Now, then, let's bustle about, or we shan't get our man in!"

The three clerks under twenty appeared to have some idea of compelling young Stansfield to attend upon them, but he pointed out that this arrangement would leave nobody to wait upon him, and he expressed a strong and decided preference for the principle of share and share alike. They gave in, robbing the act of some of its grace by pointing out that this must on no account be taken as a precedent, and that his good fortune in beginning London life on such a wonderful day did not mean that his business career would consist entirely of a beanfeast.

They also introduced him, rather severely, to certain table manners which he had not hitherto met, and he found himself greatly obstructed by a rule which prevented one from holding the leg of a fowl and dispensing with the assistance of a knife. The remains of a very fine old Stilton struck him as possessing a flavour entirely different from the American or Dutch to which he had been accustomed at home; the drawback was that you could not eat much of it.

"Do you smoke, Stansfield?"

"I'm not a slave to it!"

"You soon will be," they prophesied. "Find the matches for us."

As they puffed at their pipes, he read the financial journal spread upon the table, beginning with a casual attention, presently becoming interested. One or two points were dim to him, and he asked questions, but the others were either not completely informed, or they preferred to reserve the knowledge for private use, and they failed to explain to him why, if the newspaper people were aware that certain investments could not fail to be remunerative, the newspaper people gave the valuable tip away, instead of reserving it for their own personal benefit.

The three appeared more at home on another question, and he, having once drawn Silvio in a Derby sweepstake, could contribute something to this discussion. They told him a useful man was always to be found near the cab-rank in front of the Brighton Company's station, to whom a shilling or more could be safely confided.

The talk on this subject became animated; they gave the new lad some absolutely safe and certain news concerning a horse running in the next month, news which had come to them in a roundabout way, but starting, so they declared, from the brother of a jockey whose name they mentioned with bated breath. Young Stansfield suggested it would look well if they were to affect some engagement on business affairs; but the rest said, "Not for Joe!" They, however, agreed, very handsomely, that he could do as he pleased.

He cleared the table, filled waste-paper baskets with remnants, set desks in order, placed empty bottles out of the way. Thus he proved the only one who was giving any signs of work when Mr. Cruttwell returned, in a state of some disturbance because of news he had received concerning the prospects of one of the two opposition candidates. Mr. Cruttwell distributed blame on the others by praising young Stansfield.

"This lad is going to get on in the world!" he asserted emphatically. "I flatter myself I'm a judge of character, and I don't have to look twice at anybody. Simply disgraceful the way you youngsters loaf about and take no interest in anything but how to avoid work. Now then, set to, all of you, and follow his example. No wonder trade's so bad. I shall be in again directly, and if I find any of you lolling about I shall simply—"

They reproved the lad severely for marring an otherwise perfect day, and he hastened to inform them he had no more considerable taste for labour than that which they possessed; his only idea had been to avoid, by use of ingenuity, the disaster that had fallen upon them. He knew as well as they that nothing was to be gained by a too persistent attention to the desk, and he hoped time would succeed in persuading them he was worthy of their companionship.

They gave in reluctantly, and before the seniors returned had given him some useful hints, which he stored carefully in the recesses of his brain.

The arrangement made by his mother was that he should reach Peckham by seven o'clock, and he felt anxious to do this, for Aunt Mabel was a cheery, irresponsible person who, on her rare visits to the country, always brought a budget of amusing songs and some excellent riddles; there seemed good reason to hope that life at Peckham would be free from the close and rigid supervision exercised at home. But the others said the announcement of the election result would be the event of a lifetime, something that might never happen again, and he stayed on till a late hour, enjoying the noisy crowds and the turbulent rushes, and responding to shouted appeals for three cheers. When the poll was declared, he joined in the exultant shrieks of triumph, and a stout old lady from Long Lane insisted upon teaching him an Irish jig. Mr. Cruttwell found him, shook hands heartily, and told him the nation was perfectly sound at heart.

As he went in the direction of Peckham he found in his pocket the change given at the International Hotel. It had not been asked for, it would probably not now be asked for. Before reaching Bricklayers' Arms he came to the decision to invest a part, and to back Vendetta. A wonderful beginning!

His name was again mentioned. He stood up, gripping the bar in front of him.

"Benjamin Stansfield," recited the clerk, seated below the judge, "you are charged for that you feloniously and fraudulently—" A rumble of words. "How say you, Benjamin Stansfield: are you guilty, or not guilty?"

"Guilty!" he replied.

IV

SLOW RECOVERY

Mrs. Marchant offered a pointed remark concerning the indolent habits of London folk as compared with the early rising and the continuous industry shown by people living in the country. Called by a boy who required a weekly journal, she, without leaving the pavement, instructed him to look over the contents of the counter and help himself, adding a warning that sweets were not to be touched.

"I don't want to miss nothing" she remarked.

Her neighbour, absorbed in the subject previously under discussion, replied to the effect that there was not so much going on in Hayford that one could afford to evade incident.

"I see her blind move," screamed a small child excitedly. "I did! I see it move, quite plain."

Her elders were giving reproof, and pointing; out the risks incurred by children who told stories, when the green Venetians of the first-floor room at the Windmill Inn went, up. Interest in the one street of the village at once reawakened. A message was sent to the forge, and Sprules, the blacksmith, strolled out, drinking tea from a saucer. A tall girl stepped from the porch of the inn and whistled several times, called the word "Fuzzy!"' in varying tones of insistence and appeal. Banks, the young grocer and draper, peered through his window over columns of flannel, and then came to the doorway, where, acknowledging her salutation, he bowed and blushed.

"Morning, everybody," she said. "Any news? Has any one"

"He's been seen again, miss," remarked Sprules, setting down his saucer on a window-sill, and advancing with respect. "Old Joe Baldwin were up at four this morning, and he caught sight of your dog; somewheres, so far as I understand him, away in that direction." Sprules gave a vague flourish of his bare arm. "Consequently, you can take it from me that he aint left the neighbourhood up to the present."

The others nodded.

"Unless I find him to-day," announced the girl definitely, "I shall have to continue my journey."

They made way for Mrs. Marchant. That lady gave up her broom to gain more freedom in argument, and stepped forward.

"My dear," she said, in a motherly way, "I'm a tidy bit older than what you are, and it stands to reason I know more of the world. People come from far and wide to get my advice, they do, and none can't ever complain that I sent 'em empty away."

The rest gave a murmur that sounded like confirmation.

"Moreover, you're only a Londoner, and that sort of hampers you. My experience, my dear, tells me that it don't do to expect everything to 'appen all at once. Your dog or rather the dog belonging to a gentleman military friend that you was taking charge of slips his collar three days ago, whilst your train was stoppin' at the station, .and makes off. You, being tur'bly upset, you gives up your journey, and you offers ten shillin' reeward. On my suggestion, you next day makes it two pound. Still acting on my racommendation, you, the foiring day, increases it to five."

"That is more than I can really afford." "Never you mind 'bout that," said the other, with a touch of impatience. "I'm only tellin' you what happened. I'm a business woman, and I like to have everything straight for'ard, and above board. I know all that occurs in Hayford, and if you leave yourself in my hands, you won't go fur wrong. Your dog's been seen, and that ought to be enough for you, to go on with."

"If he could only catch sight of me, he'd come directly. Fuzzy is as fond of me as he is of his master."

"But not near so fond, miss, I lay a pint," interposed Sprules, with a wink to the others, "as what his master is of you."

She regarded him with a steady gaze; the blacksmith tried to hum a tune, and failing in this, mentioned it was high time he went back to finish his breakfast.

"I have been walking around the neighbourhood," the girl went on, "every day in the hope of finding him, and I haven't succeeded. To-night, by the 6.37, I must go on, and—" with a break in her voice, "I shall have to face Captain Stamford."

"My dear," said Mrs. Marchant encouragingly, "you make it ten, and some 'ing seems to tell me you'll get your dog back."

"That would mean giving up my holiday," she answered doubtfully. Young Banks, draper and grocer, stepped forward: some one pulled at his apron. "But if you think it will increase the efforts of the villagers, I'll do as you suggest."

"Ten pound," announced Mrs. Marchant, addressing the others in tones of authority, "to any one what brings this lady's dog back here to The Windmill afore six o'clock this very evening."

The small crowd broke up. Children were sent off to school, and instructed in audible voices to keep a wary look-out for Fuzzy. The constable came from his headquarters at a neighbouring village, and was told of the increase in the reward; he went on to communicate the information, far and near. Mrs. Marchant took the cork from a bottle of red ink and made a correction in the hand-written bill headed "Lost, Stolen or Strayed" that rested on a box of caramels in her window. At half -past nine the London girl in a brown costume with a conveniently short skirt and carrying a walking-stick, left The Windmill and strode off in a northerly direction, the landlord wishing her, with great heartiness, good luck in her search; she sang out that she would return for tea. Ten minutes' grace, and a meeting was held near to the porch of the tavern, with Mrs. Marchant in a standing position, but obviously in the chair. She glanced around at the four men present.

"Some one go for Mr. Banks," she ordered.

Sprules took charge of the task, and returned with the message that the young draper and grocer was making up his books; Banks had suggested the deliberation should go on as though he were present.

"I don't want to complain of nobody," commented Mrs. Marchant, "but Mr. Banks don't seem to take the interest in public affairs like what he ought to do. How-so-ever," dismissing this point, "what we've got to consider now is whether we've come to what they call in the newspapers the crucial moment, or whether we ought to go on a bit further."

"Young party seems fairly bent on getting away this evening," remarked the owner of The Windmill. "In fact, I may tell you all she's settled up her bill."

"My idea is," said Sprules, "that we've arrived at the limit. Enough is as good as a feast."

"Is the dog all right?" asked Mrs. Marchant.

"Safe and sound," replied the blacksmith, "where it's been since it first slipped the collar. And I hope you won't none of you forget that I've had to bear the axpense of feeding it."

"That amounts to a mere trifle," commented Mrs. Marchant curtly. "From what I know of you, Mr. Sprules, I'll be bound you ent overdone it."

"What might you mean by that, ma'am?"

"I mean what I say."

"A civil question," persisted Sprules, "requires a civil answer."

"You've come to the wrong shop for that,"

retorted the lady, with increasing heat.

"When I speak, I speak plain, I do. If you must know what I was driving at it was that, 'cording to all reports, you're the only one in your 'ouse who enjoys a hearty meal. What you can't eat, you give to your wife and the children."

The proprietor of The Windmill, an experienced man in the settlement of disputes by arbitration, and one frequently called upon to decide knotty points (such as the exact height of the late Lord Randolph Churchill, or the winner of the Oaks in '94) found some trouble in bringing the discussion back to the item on the agenda. Before he succeeded in effecting this, Sprules had managed to tell Mrs. Marchant what he thought of her, and Mrs. Marchant told Sprules what she thought of him. Even when the original topic was again approached, the two eyed each other from opposite sides of the pavement; their lips continued to move without producing words.

"No occasion to quarrel," said the inn-keeper soothingly. "The amount ent large enough to justify that. When it's all divided out equally."

The tumult recommenced, and Mr. Banks, leaving his books, came to his doorway, a pen over each ear; he seemed tempted to give up business for pleasure, but, with an effort, returned to his shop. This time Mrs. Marchant and Sprules found themselves, by the" sport of circumstances, in agreement; the rest, with the exception of the proprietor of The Windmill, nodded approval of their contention. The Windmill, they argued, had made a good profit out of the young lady; The Windmill must take this fact into consideration in formulating its claim. Fair was fair, all the world over. Similarly, right was right, no matter where you lived. The proprietor of The Windmill, almost in tears, declared that his habit was to charge customers the merest trifle over cost price; an error in addition had, he told them, been detected by the young lady in settling the account. Perceiving that the general sense of the meeting was against him, he mentioned that he had no desire to become unpopular, and he therefore left himself in their hands.

"By the by," remarked some one, "didn't the young party buy a couple of old brass candlesticks from Mr. Banks's mother?"

The fact had escaped memory, but only this hint was necessary to recall it. It was not known how much had been paid for the articles, but the village felt justified in assuming they were not given away, and the question was how much ought to be deducted. Foreheads took additional wrinkles at the prospect of mental arithmetic, and Sprules had found, in his pocket, a short stump of wood which was once a pencil, when Mrs. Marchant, lowering her voice, made a proposition which instantly met with a chorus of approval. Young Banks had taken little or no share in the whole business; he was evidently entitled to no share in the profits. Young Banks, a strict Wesleyan, had, in the hearing of one, characterised the affair as shady, and he could scarcely object to being left out. It was agreed that nothing should be said to young Banks for the present, and the meeting broke up with smiles, expressions of mutual regard, warning fingers that urged secrecy. A small sub-committee went to inspect the captive dog at the back of Sprules's forge.

Mr. Banks was noticed to be giving instructions at two o'clock that afternoon to his assistant: a few minutes later shutters went up and Banks, straw-hatted, and carrying a light cane, went off, at a good pace, as one determined to enjoy a long walk. The assistant, answering inquiries, said the procedure was in the nature of an experiment, and could be taken as part and parcel of the Early Closing scheme. At four o'clock Sprules brought out Fuzzy, and tied the defiant-looking Irish terrier to the anvil; in the forge, Sprules rehearsed to a smoked portrait of Mr. Gladstone, tacked on the wall, an account of the capture of Fuzzy, to be given to the young woman upon her return. Sprules was in the third repetition of this (for improvements occurred to him) when his name was called. He unfastened the dog and took it out, shading eyes with the disengaged hand from the afternoon sun.

"I'm oncommon glad to inform you, miss, that our efforts have at last—Oh, it's you, Mr. Banks!"

"Yes," said the young draper and grocer, "it's me. I happened to meet the lady up near Watbury, and she asked me to come back here, to save her the walk, and to see about sending on her portmanteau. She's found her dog."

"She's done what?"

"You know them nut trees as you go down the hill, on the left-hand side? Just beyond the bridge I mean. Extraordinary pleased about it, she is, naturally. And Fuzzy, of course, half off his head at seeing her again."

"Mr. Banks," said the blacksmith, distressedly, "let's get this all clear. Do I onder stand from you that the dog I've got here, at the end of this piece of string, isn't the animal the reeward was offered for?"

"The lady only lost one."

Sprules rubbed the top of his head. Mr. Banks patted the dog, and tried to induce it to stand on its hind legs.

"Then what's to be done with this yer animal? I've got no use for him. 'Sides which, he tried all he knew just now to bite me."

"I've got an aunt living down the line," said young Banks, regarding the dog critically, "and I owe her a birthday present. I had intended to give about five shilling for something."

"The dog's yourn!" said the blacksmith promptly.

Mr. Banks carried the portmanteau off in good time for the 6.37, and the dog, with a label bearing the address of his relative, went with him. At the station, he made an alteration in the wording of the label, and took the ticket for it that is furnished when a dog accompanies a passenger. There were no other customers for the train, and he and the one porter had an animated discussion concerning the new minister whose name was on the plan to take up duties shortly. The train came in; the porter went to the brake van to see to arriving luggage.

"You dear old Fuzzy!" cried the girl delightedly, as the dog with a single bound jumped into her compartment. "Mr. Banks, how can I thank you, and how much do I owe you?"

She took charge of the portmanteau, and opened her purse.

"You don't owe me nothing," replied young Banks, reddening. The engine whistled. "But if you want to pay me, and you think your friend Captain Stamford wouldn't object, you might you might jest blow me a kiss as the train goes out!"

V

LOOSE CASH

A Prince of Wales was born, and Mr. Rollinson re-christened a row of houses which he had acquired. The original builder had gone incautiously on a certain evening in the early part of '41 to inspect his property an act nobody else thought of performing and stumbled into one of the numerous holes that lined the approach. His widow found herself unable to carry on the building operations, and Mr. Rollinson, who, owing to popular prejudice, had just given up a career on the turf and some profitable transactions near the prize ring, offered her two hundred pounds ready cash for the lot.

"Could you make it two fifty, Mr. Rollinson?"

"I'll make it three hundred, because I like your manner."

"Oh, you dear good generous soul!" she cried.

He paid in rather greasy-looking bank-notes, and, later on, married her, and thus secured a return of the amount.

The Albert Edward estate was announced as specially suitable for newly married people, and these came, in pairs, attracted by the title and by the health statistics of the neighbourhood; a few carping critics pointed out that the agreeable figures were due to the sparsity of the population, but no one troubled to follow the argument. Meanwhile Mr. Rollinson ordered that building should go on with haste to meet the demands of would-be tenants, who, by an ingenious scheme of payments, became in a term of years responsible owners of the property, and he only relinquished the task when children began to arrive and the dwellings, in consequence, showed signs of wear and tear. He then went to Finsbury Park, and laid out the Princess Alice estate; later he proceeded to Hammersmith, and planned and carried out the Duke of Edinburgh estate. These houses might be exhibited at the present day, a tribute to Rollinson's loyalty and industry, but for the interference of borough officials. By the time these steps were taken, Mr. Rollinson had disengaged himself from interest in the various properties, but one can understand the pain given by the action of the authorities to a man whose official letter paper bore the heading, "Not for an Age, but for all Time."

Ernest Napoleon, the son, was born in '43, and the event is registered at the church in Hart Street, Bloomsbury; his father, despite activities concerning new dwellings, preferred to reside in an older quarter of town. Mr. Rollinson found tune to take a part in public life, and I have ascertained that he was one of 170,000 special constables sworn in at the time of the threatened Chartist riots; unfortunately, on the day of the meeting at Kennington Common, he was suffering from a slight headache, and he advised his neighbour, Dr. Fennell, to order him to stay in bed. Friendship between himself and his medical man increased as Mr. Rollinson spoke of his fortunate investments.

"Want you to dome a great favour, George," asked Dr. Fennell, meeting him one day near the Museum. "My idea is that I ought very soon to be able to retire, and cultivate a garden in the country. But progress in my profession is slow."

"You're as safe as 'ouses," remarked Mr. Rollinson, "safe as some 'ouses, I mean providing you're not fool enough to go in for speculation."

"Speculation," declared the doctor warmly, "is the last vice I should indulge in. All I want you to do, the next time you see a good thing in prospect, is just to let me come in with you. I've five thousand pounds put by, and call me ambitious, or what you will I should like to make it ten. Promise me you'll do your best."

"Can't guarantee success, mind you."

"My dear George," protested the other, "give me credit for a fair amount of common sense."

The Great Exhibition was a year or two distant, but preparations were already being made, and Mr. Rollinson heard of several investments in regard to it that promised well; a scheme for obtaining all the printing work sounded so excellent that he brought it to the notice of his friend; the drawback was that only five thousand pounds appeared to be required. On Fennell's earnest appeal he agreed to stand aside, and allow the doctor to take full advantage of the opportunity.

"But don't you go forgetting that I warned you there was a risk."

"Nothing venture, George," said Fennell contentedly, "nothing have!"

When the auction took place in Bloomsbury Square, Mr. Rollinson acting, so it was rumoured, from motives of generosity towards an old and valued friend overtaken by misfortune, made arrangements with dealers, and purchased nearly all of Dr. Fennell's furniture. He also bought the remainder of the lease. The goodwill he obtained at a fair price, and sold at another, and the ground floor was let to a new man who was told to keep the practice going for sixteen or eighteen years.

"What's the idea of arranging that, Mr. R.?" asked his wife respectfully.

"Don't you ask questions," he retorted, "I'm looking well ahead!"

"If it's something in store for our boy, I'm quite satisfied."

"It is something for my boy, but I don't care a hang whether you are satisfied or not."

"Do you think we ought to get a governess in for him, Mr. R.?"

"I shall take charge of his education, and I don't want no one interferin'. I'm a going to have him brought up proper, so as he'll turn out to be a credit to me, later on. And, although it's got nothing to do with you, I don't mind mentioning that trouble will be no object. No object, whatsoever. I've got along pretty well without much beyond readin' and writin' and figurin', and it stands to reason he'll have a better chance than what I did, if he's fitted out more complete. But don't you go putting your spoke in, or else me and you'll have words. Quite enough for you that he's going to be brought up to be a doctor and a gentleman. Especially a gentleman!"

Although the printing scheme had ended in disaster, owing to the action of a mysterious gentleman in the City, there were others of a more solid nature in connection with the Hyde Park show, and it was said at this time that it was only necessary for Mr. Rollinson to be mixed up in any transaction to ensure success, so far as he was concerned. Some might endure stabs at the hand of Fortune, but Rollinson always came through safely. Often times his name did not appear, and knowing folk therefore multiplied his gains by twenty to make sure they were well within the mark.

We are now at '51.

It was during this year that the boy Ernest first gained special attention, and caused his father's pride to increase. Mrs. Rollinson, with the improvement in income, and aided by a dressmaker of Theobald's Road, cultivated a definite note in apparel, and her favourite costume was one of a tartan pattern, full in the flounces and so tightly stayed at the waist that the poor lady's complexion was sometimes scarlet, sometimes purple. At the start, she had, for motives of economy, herself made the child's clothes, but the boy reported to his father that these, by reason of their amplitude—

"You must allow for growing," urged his mother.

These caused him to become the object of ridicule, and his father at once put a stop to home manufactures. Ernest, thereafter, during Exhibition year, wore suits of velvet with frilled knickerbockers, and a stiffly carded cap with a blue tassel dependent, and his appearance extorted nothing but admiration as he walked, hand-iii-hand with his father, along the transept of Mr. Joseph Paxton's great building of glass. The boy had been furnished with several facts and arguments in connection with the place, and these he recited in a clear, distinct voice.

"Looking around, dear papa, at this striking scene, it seems impossible to think that war will again occur in our time."

And,

"I believe this immense building covers twenty acres of ground, and is no less than two thousand feet long. Please correct me, papa, if I am in error."

Quite distinguished -looking ladies and gentlemen took notice of the boy's intelligence, and some gave him fourpenny pieces, patting him on the cap, and telling him he was a fine little fellow; a well-known politician prophesied of him, on one occasion, that he would grow up to be an Englishman in the best sense of the word. You can imagine Mr. Rollinson's delight at these compliments, and the satisfaction in finding his own views confirmed from responsible quarters. It was his method, in regard to domestic affairs, to ascertain Mrs. Rollinson's wishes and then to give instructions that the exact opposite should be adopted, but, returning home after one of these gratifying afternoons in Hyde Park, he took the unusual course of inviting her to his study, where, in smoking-cap and dressing-gown (a change from the restraint of out-door clothes) he bade her take the easy-chair, whilst he himself stood near the empty fireplace and leaned an elbow on the mantelpiece, in an attitude imposed by more than one artist upon the Prince Consort.

"You will no doubt say, Mrs. Rollinson," he remarked, "that making money as I do now, and not doing much work for it, we ought to go on a steppin' up the ladder. Allow me to remind you that sometimes I don't retain all the cash I receive. Sounds peculiar, but it's a fact. I find the money that takes the most trouble to get is the money that stays with me longest. Putting that all aside, your view, womanlike, is that we've only got one life to live in this world, whatever 'appens to us in the next, and that we're entitled to make the most of it. You'll tell me that we both of us had a hard time in the early days, and we're justified in claiming our reward. And mind you, there's something in your argument."

Mrs. Rollinson, much astonished at this commendation of her presumed opinions, could find no words either to protest or to agree. She smoothed her crimped hair and bowed.

"But perhaps," he went on in the same amazing tones of deference, "perhaps you won't mind if I point out that we're living now in a very fair state of comfort. We have roast meat every other day; if you feel inclined to go now and again to see Mr. Wigan at the St. James's, why, you've only got to say so. And this brings me to the point of what I'm talking about. Why shouldn't we go on as we're going now, not wasting money specially, not 'oarding it to any special degree, but going a reg'lar buster in regard to the boy? Giving him chances that his father never had, seeing that he has every opportunity of growing up so that he can take his place amongst the 'ighest of the land? Now then, Mrs. R.! If you've got anything further to remark on the subject, here's the time to say it, or ever after hold your peace."

"Sometimes," she ventured to remark, "you've pitched into me and told me I was spoiling him."

"There's a right way of doing it," he retorted, "and a wrong way of doing it."

"And you've said, more than once, that to make a man of him he ought to go through the mill, same as what you did."

"There again, there's two ways open."

"If you can find the right way, Mr. R., I'm perfectly agreeable."

"You're a wise woman," he declared, "although very often you manage to conceal the fact. And I promise you faithfully that if you leave it all to me, you won't have no reason to be sorry!"

Ernest grew up tall, slim, good-looking, and with fair, curly hair; it was therefore reckoned impossible to make him a doctor. Apart from this, he showed no special intelligence, and at the new military college at Sandhurst the masters said caustically it was a pity the lad had not been born in America, for then the Civil War there would have been of very short duration. Discouraged by these comments, Ernest, of his own accord, left the College, thus depriving the British army of his services, and, coming back to town, took rooms in Jermyn Street, and mentioned to his father and mother that he proposed to look about him, a task which it is well known cannot be done in a hurry. Money was supplied from Bloomsbury Square, and it appeared to have some peculiar quality, for it all slipped through Ernest's fingers with the greatest possible ease. Having, in spite of his defects, an amiable disposition, he soon found acquaintances, mainly amongst other men who were also looking about, and when they discovered he had money at his command, and that his cheques were always after sometimes a brief delay honoured, their admiration of his qualities knew no bounds.

"You've got a simple manner," they said, "but, by gad, underneath that there's any amount of cunning and cleverness."

"Eeally think so?" inquired Ernest, pleased.

"Enough for ten ordinary people," they declared. "Got a fi'pun note about you?"

Also, they gave him sound advice in regard to keeping well in with the governor: a dinner was arranged at a club to which one of them belonged, and, at the expense of Ernest, Mr. Rollinson was entertained, and made much of; Wilner (who had been twice through the Bankruptcy Court, using up several pails of whitewash and coming out not quite clean) Wilner made a speech, proposing old Rollinson's health, declaring that their guest was one of the bulwarks of the nation, and that his well-equipped son would, later on, when he had finished looking about, become one of the foremost men in the State. Privately, Wilner told Mr. Rollinson that all our best politicians had sown their wild oats in early days, and gave an amusing and little-known anecdote concerning a member of the Cabinet.

"What he wants," said old Rollinson, glancing at his son, "is concentration, if you know what it means, sir. "

"That will grow on him," remarked the other lightly. "All he has to do just now is to make plenty of friends. And it isn't for a mere amateur like myself to give advice to an experienced man of the world like George Rollinson."

Oddly enough, the term had never before been applied to him. Old Rollinson fixed his cigar at a more rakish angle.

"But if I were you, I should see that, for a year or two at any rate, he was not stinted of money." Wilner gazed reflectively at his glass of claret. "I've seen so many youngsters, fine, promising, delightful lads, go to the deuce just for want of a few paltry hundreds. And you needn't begrudge it, you know. By all accounts you make it easily enough."

The rest of the dinner-party, once they had, as Wilner neatly phrased it, put off the old man, went to the Argyll Rooms, and later to Bob Croft's in the Hay market (no use in going to Croft's until midnight), where Ernest insisted upon playing the harp, with the aid of his walking-stick; when the police came to make their usual nightly round, Ernest demanded the company of the Inspector in the Varsoviana. Wilner and the others were satisfied with the efforts of their pupil and allowed him, at his special request, to pay for everything. This was the occasion when Ernest lighted a cigar with one of the notes given to him by his father, and found some difficulty in making the paper burn.

There were times when Ernest, troubled with remorse and a severe headache, spoke of giving it all up, and returning to Bloomsbury Square; the bodyguard had to use their best powers of derision. An accusation of want of pluck generally proved effective; later, a slip of the pen on the part of Ernest gave them a better hold, and they had only to draw his attention to the punishment awarded by the law for forgery. Old Rollinson fell ill, in consequence of a chill sustained on the steam-boat returning from Greenwich after his new doctor had ordered him a sea voyage, and the remittances stopped. A new and promising-looking pigeon flew into the district of the Circus; Wilner and his colleagues dropped the acquaintance of Ernest, who could find no better companion than a wise young housemaid at Jermyn Street. The girl gave him good advice and went with him to Bloomsbury Square, waiting at the railings whilst he entered to see his father, to make frank avowals, and to impersonate the prodigal son. He came out in less than half an hour, and it seemed at once evident that the fatted calf was still alive.

"Says I've disappointed him," reported Ernest tearfully, "and that he never wants to see me again. Declares he did his best for me, and all I've done has been to spend nearly every penny he gained, and there's nothing to show for it, excepting a good-for-nothing, broken-down young man. And mother agreed with him. "

"Appears to me," remarked Helen, "some one is going to have the responsibility of looking after you."

"I wish you'd marry me."

"That will be about the best plan," she agreed.

Ernest Rollinson died in '64, and soon after the old people went. Young Mrs. Rollinson, putting her baby boy away with some working people in Clerkenwell, entered service again.

A Home for Indigent Bookmakers found itself benefited by the terms of the Bloomsbury Square will; nothing was left to the son's family, in spite of the device used in christening the baby. Helen worked hard in her good situation and saved money, paying the folk in Corporation Lane weekly, and now and again snatching an hour off to see her boy. She was there one afternoon in December watching with amusement his celebrated impersonation of a policeman on the track of a Fenian (he had some new piece of cleverness each time she paid her furtive visits) when a tremendous clatter came from the wall of the prison opposite, the house trembled, plaster of the ceiling fell in a thick white shower, and then the place collapsed. Helen Rollinson found herself pulled out of the debris and screamed loudly for her George; they brought to her a maimed child, and she, almost demented, was nursing the poor thing in the confusion of the street, and begging it not to die, when Master George himself trotted up, safe and sound, demanding of his mother whether she had noticed the splendid fireworks. She placed the injured child in the hands of one of the doctors, heard that the woman of the house was not expected to recover, and rushed away with her boy from the disastrous scene.

"Well for you, Helen," said her excellent mistress, "that you are able to show me your marriage lines, otherwise it would be my duty, as a strict Churchwoman, to turn you out of the house, neck and crop. As it is, you have practised deceit on me, and I am afraid we must look upon this dreadful affair at Clerkenwell as a judgment for your sin."

"They seemed to suspect some Irish people, ma'am."

"Heaven has its own way of punishing evil-doers," declared the lady, "and it isn't for us to question its methods. You cannot stay here any longer."

"I must find another situation, I s'pose, ma'am. But I shan't get such a good one as this."

"Deceit," insisted the other, "is one of the things that must, on no account, be encouraged. What is your boy like?"

The child, brought from the kitchen, repeated for the benefit of Helen's mistress his account of the explosion, a performance that had been well received downstairs. The lady was impressed.

"A clever boy," she said. "Would you like me to adopt him, Helen, and thus leave you free?''

"I'd rather starve than let him go away from me again."

"Supposing, then," said the lady, getting over her surprise at this attitude, "supposing I set you up in a small business of some kind; will you promise me never to be deceitful again? ' Helen gave the required guarantee, and her mistress put the small boy through a viva-voce examination; his replies concerning the award meted out to naughty people fortunately coincided exactly with the lady's own views.

Helen Rollinson, widow of Ernest Rollinson, and mother of George Rollinson, saw her name painted over a shop in Southampton Row, with the words added, on either side of the main inscription, "Newsagent" and "Tobacconist"; she let the rooms above, giving some personal attendance, used the apartment at the back of the shop as a living-room whence she could see when a customer entered, occupied spare moments by making clothes for George, preparing necessary meals, and telling him to be a good lad. She slept for about six hours every night, giving the remaining eighteen to hard work, and to the considerable task of minding her own business. Mr. Forster carried his Education Act just in time to enable George to take advantage of it, and the boy was one of the earliest to pay sixpence a week and become a pupil of the State at a superior school; in his spare time he delivered newspapers and ran errands, sometimes going so far as the City and making use of the new Viaduct at Holborn; he was at first terrified by these important missions, but overhearing his mother speak of him to a customer as a boy who knew his way about, he determined to keep his fears to himself, and to overcome them. Moreover, there was the knowledge that undertakings of the kind, perilous as they might be, saved expense. Mrs. Rollinson watched every penny, every halfpenny, and spoke with genuine regret when disbursements had to be made to the Parcels Delivery Company.

"Throwing away good money!" she declared.

She explained to George, in answer to his question, a theory she held in regard to the coinage of the United Kingdom, and he embodied these views in an essay at school the following morning. His teacher, greatly diverted, read the paper aloud to the class, and the boys followed the lead, glad of an excuse for boisterous amusement. George flushed, and kept his head down. It gives some notion of the difficulties experienced by the State in its early days of keeping school when I mention that George ranged himself on the side of his parent, and declined to accept the opinions of educational authorities; the teacher, noting his attitude, spoke to him later in the playground, and assured him again that his argument was based upon error. Money, said the teacher, was manufactured at a place called the Mint situated east of the City; the gold coins were actual value, whilst the rest were called tokens, representing a value only by agreement. Notes were made on special paper, and printed under the supervision of the Bank of England. To write, as George Rollinson had done, that there were two kinds of money, one dry and the other slippery, one easy to retain and the other impossible to keep, was to make an assertion that, in the light of facts, could not possibly be supported.

"So get that nonsensical idea out of your head, my lad," advised his teacher earnestly, "as soon as you possibly can. You have a good deal to learn yet, remember."

On most subjects George accepted the instructions of the representatives of the State, bringing home to Southampton Row items of geographical information and snips of historical news; his mother nodded approvingly and hinted that all the particulars had once been learnt by her, but, owing to pressure of other matters, forgotten. When the boy asked about his father she constructed for his encouragement, and her own content, an ideal man, dogged, wise, and industrious, never wasting a moment of valuable time, always thrifty. Upon George inquiring why, in these circumstances, they had not been left more comfortably off, she fell back on her old theory regarding cash, and told him in conclusion that little boys who did not ask too many questions would find their appropriate reward in not being told too many lies.

The profits of the business were small, but they were sure. The newspaper and magazine side increased slightly year by year with nothing in the nature of a set-back, excepting the occasional defalcation of some customer with a poor memory, and lightly furnished in the way of luggage. Mrs. Rollinson, when the lad was of a sufficient age, showed him the results of the business, and George said they ought to sell letter paper at the tobacco counter, seeing that the figures there were stationary. Mrs. Rollinson gave this remark as "George's latest" to a customer, a short, clean-shaven man, who patronised the shop for lucifer matches, and the customer pronounced it good; later, in calling, he mentioned he had worked it into a burlesque at the Strand Theatre where he was playing, and that it went fairly well. He added that he had never yet found the perfect tobacco, and now almost despaired of doing so; described the different flavours which he desired. George, listening from the shop parlour, asked permission of his mother to make a few experiments; she gave her consent, on the understanding that there should be no waste. The results, tried in the celebrated actor's pipe, gained emphatic approval, and George suggested a letter should be written from the Theatre embodying these compliments and bearing a signature. The letter was framed, set in the window. Within a week Mrs. Rollinson found herself compelled to engage the services of an assistant on the tobacco side, a worthy, well-favoured man who thenceforth for many years, in accepting his wages on Saturday nights, made a proposal of marriage to her. Mrs. Rollinson declined, in set form, on the grounds that she wished to look after George.

"Very well then," he would say resignedly. "Then I s'pose I must wait."

On a Saturday when George brought a young lady from High Street, Marylebone, to the shop, and introduced her to his mother with the remark, "I want you two to be friends!" Mrs. Rollinson, greatly upset, perturbed the assistant by giving in reply to the usual question an unusual answer. He went out of the shop in a dazed condition, and on the Monday morning a letter came from him, stating that, on reflection, he decided he was unworthy of the great honour, and he hoped Mrs. Rollinson would not mind if, instead, he sailed for Canada.

"It's all for the best!" said Mrs. Rollinson. After going to chapel twice on the intervening Sunday, she was regarding the possibility of the engagement of her son with greater calm. "George will have to work harder, and I'm good for several years yet. We shall rub along all right. He needn't get married until he's thirty. It's quite fashionable nowadays for gentlemen to wait until they're getting on in life."

She told him that her first criticism of the girl had been made on the impulse of the moment: she now begged to withdraw the word "minx" and to substitute a more flattering noun.

"Very glad to hear you say that, mother. She's a girl with most wonderful ideas in her head."

"That doesn't matter," replied Mrs. Rollinson tolerantly, "So long as she leaves them there."

"What I mean is, extraordinarily ambitious."

"I'm like that, too," she remarked. "I've set my 'eart on having the front of the shop done up this spring. Me and her will get on hapitally together. Make your mind quite easy. She can come here every Christmas day and now and again on Sundays but not too often-and when eventually you get married, why, if all goes well, I'll retire and I'll leave you the business. Can't say fairer than that can I?"

"Mother," the lad blurted out, "she wanted it to be a secret for a time, but I can't keep it back from you. We're married already!"

"No, George, my boy. That isn't true, surely!"

" I take all the responsibility," he went on, "but she said it was no use letting the grass grow under our feet."

"I wish," said Mrs. Rollinson aside, to the negro figure in the corner, "that grass was growing over her head!"

This was the final word of a vehement nature that George's mother used in regard to her daughter-in-law. When she took some of the furniture, and rode away on the tail of the van to Chalk Farm, she told the middle aged man with the green baize apron that there was nothing like retiring from business whilst one was still capable of enjoying life: to the lady who owned the house where the furniture was unloaded she mentioned, in taking possession of the two rooms on the ground floor, that her only visitors would be her son and her son's wife; she hoped they would be in and out of the place frequently. Mrs. Rollinson gave a short, enthusiastic description of the bride and remarked that she already looked upon the girl as her own daughter.

"It'll be a comfort to me, ma'am," said the landlady mournfully, "to have a merry party about the house. The only thing is I don't mean anything personal but I've generally found that when parties were cheerful, they turned out to be rather bad payers."

Mrs. Rollinson produced her pass-book; exhibited figures showing the balance to her credit.

"That's good enough," said the other, with something like rapture. She was leaving the room, but curiosity detained her at the edge of the carpet. "You must have had some rare strokes of luck, in your day, ma'am!"

Mrs. Rollinson shook her head resolutely. "It's all been saved out of hard work," she declared.

"I was half hoping," remarked the landlady, relapsing into gloom, "it was a case of easy come, easy go!"

The expected callers did not arrive on the first Sunday afternoon, although tea was prepared, crumpets ready, and Mrs. Rollinson had rehearsed several amiable speeches to be addressed to her daughter-in-law. So soon as it became dusk she walked down to Southampton Row, and from the opposite side of the roadway took a view. The shop was shuttered, and, alarmed by this Sunday evening was one of the best times for receipts she crossed, and read the notice. Retail Department Closed, said the bills. Central Office of the English Tobacco Syndicate. Branches all over the Country. Capital and here so many figures (mainly noughts) that Mrs. Rollinson could not reckon them.

"Slippery money," she said, on the way home. She paid the cabman in threepenny pieces, and he remarked that she might as well also hand over the offertory bag.

Young Mrs. George Rollinson delayed her call for nearly two years, and then she had no occasion to pay a fare; her manner when, on leaving Chalk Farm, she said to the coach-man "Home, Watson!"

Was, in itself, proof of the ease with which cultured habits can be acquired by those who set their minds to the task. Before going she, prefacing by the remark that she had called for a quiet chat, spoke at length and with great rapidity. They were living, George and herself, up West; Mrs. Rollinson observed that the exact address was not tendered, and a return call was evidently unnecessary. The present scheme was going on remarkably well, astonishingly well, amazingly well, and young Mrs. Rollinson had special cause for gratification in that it originated with her. For various reasons that her mother-in-law would not understand, if explained, the present scheme had taken the place of the old one, and a still newer one was in contemplation. George and his City friends knew how to manage these affairs to the best advantage. Unfortunately, it seemed likely the public might exhibit a certain reticence when the new idea was submitted to them, and investors would only become eager when they discovered that the shares, or most of them, had been privately subscribed. Just as many people only wanted to go to theatres where the notice "House Full" was exhibited, so some did not apply for shares unless they anticipated difficulty in procuring them.

"And George," said young Mrs. Rollinson, refastening her fur coat, "is anxious to show he had not forgotten you, and he asked me to say that, for the sake of old times, he is quite willing to let you take up."

"You tell George," interrupted his mother, "that whenever the time arrives that he wants to be kept out of the workhouse, he can come along to me!

I think I said something in approval of young Mrs. Rollinson's manner of giving instructions to her coachman. To be exact, it ought to be mentioned that there was a distinct trace of asperity in her tones.

Young Mrs. Rollinson said "Home, Watson!" on a good many occasions, and at various places, before the one evening when she gave to the coachman a different destination; the two well-matched horses broke down the austere behaviour of a life-time by winking at each other. George arrived at Chalk Farm by yellow omnibus, that night, after his mother had gone to rest in the back room; she came out with no indication of surprise, and started at once to make up a bed for him on the sofa. He seemed inclined to retain possession of his silk hat, partly that he might gaze into it as he gave halting explanations, but his mother wrested this from him, and ordered him to make himself at home.

"I never heard for certain," she said, when he had come to an end of the list of disasters, "but are there any children?"

George shook his head negatively.

"That's just as well," she remarked, with cheerfulness. "Now promise me, George, before we settle anything else: don't divorce her."

"I'm willing to give you my word, mother."

"Good!" she said. "That means the trouble is over. No more Rollinsons will have to undergo the test. Other people will, but not a Rollinson. Something seems to tell me that I shall out-live you, and I shall make it my business to see that you earn honestly every penny you require."

The single worry that came later was when Merry Hampton won the Derby. Mrs. Rollinson allowed George one speculation a year in the form of a half-crown ticket for a sweep-stake; prospects of success appeared sufficiently remote. George, on the canal bridge in High Street, was exhibiting to a friend his winnings when the sovereigns slipped through his fingers, and disappeared in the water below. The friend, taking the situation with great good-humour, remarked that it looked like a case of *felo s. d.*

VI

PRICE OF JAMES McWINTER

They came separately, and rather stealthily, to the restaurant in Little Compton Street, giving a cautious look up and down the street before entering. Many folk in Soho wear the brims of soft hats flattened down over eyes, carry hands deep in overcoat pockets, and walk close to shop windows, hesitating slightly before turning a corner. The restaurant patrons did not belong to this type. Some of the early-comers spoke to a constable, and said, exhibiting an envelope, because they mistrusted their French accent:

"Which do you reckon now is my best way to get to this address?"

The policeman, pointing a gloved hand to the large window that had muslin curtains of the previous summer, replied:

"If you ain't careful, sir, it'll bite you." The constable, after the first inquiries, was able to recognise the type and, interrupting the question, indicated the doorway silently with a nod of his helmet without interrupting the task of slapping his shoulder; he mentioned to an anxious younger colleague who came up and put an inquiry that they were not in his opinion so much Anarchists as country gents out on the spree. Inside the Restaurant Chicot the head waiter had also gained experience, and, as the visitors arrived, he said, "Mr. Aumairst, yes?" and with a bow led the way to a long table, that had originally been three, at the end of the large room. Chairs leaned forward in the attitude of saying grace, and these were pulled back by the head waiter, whilst a short page-boy stood on tiptoe to assist the guests in removing overcoats, mufflers, and hats. Guarded salutations "Hullo, Burnham, old man! What sort of an east wind blew you in here?" and newcomers examined the menu card with a puzzled air, giving it all up after a cursory examination excepting the plum-pudding item, and joined the rest in taking a seat and in looking over the shoulder. "I'd no notion we were to be all of us invited. What's the idea?"

"H. A." was the reply, in confident tones. "H. A. knows what he's up to."

"I quite feel that about him. Apart from liking to show off, and not being able to afford to do it, old Amherst is no fool. But whilst I know that he knows what he's up to, I can't say that I always know what he knows about knowing See what I mean, don't you? Is this him, in the Russian-bear costume?"

Mr. Amherst, in a brand-new fur-lined overcoat, was scarcely the man to deprive the public of a full view of it, and he resisted the page-boy's attempt to take possession at the door. Diners at other tables glanced up. Two matronly ladies at the corner said something in a foreign language and suspended the rule which orders that one should not laugh at one's own jokes. Men gave their closer attention to the trim young figure in a small sealskin cap and warm costume who followed so soon as Mr. Amherst 's whirling arms made it safe to do so.

"Gentlemen," he said, advancing to the long table, with the air of making a speech, "I have to apologise for being somewhat late on the Rialto, so to speak, but you've met my daughter. Waiter, another chair!" They rose, and she nodded pleasantly, giving to one her muff, another her cloak, a third her gloves. "I particularly wanted her to come along, and it occupied some little time to induce her to obey my request. She's all I've got now, you see." He sat down heavily at the top of the table. "Now then, my lad," to the attendant, in a pained manner, "we all seem to be waiting, except you. How much longer before the soup comes?"

Miss Amherst, at the other end of the table, explained to neighbours that her father's account was inexact in certain particulars. What had really happened was that she found he intended her to stop at the hotel and dine alone.

"He generally gets his own way," remarked one.

"Not if it happens to differ from mine," she said.

"Did he tell you, by any chance," lowering voices, and speaking confidentially, "what the motive was for asking us all here this evening? '

"I understood it was that you should eat a dinner." They shook their heads to convey that the information was not complete, and followed her lead in the management of the whitebait.

Near Mr. Amherst, the talk, managed and directed by him, was devoted to the political situation. The host submitted a practical method of solving the difficulty of which he spoke as one owning the patent rights; put more briefly than he explained it, it was to convey the principal members of the party with which he was not in agreement to Newgate on a convenient Monday morning, and hang them, one after the other. Near Miss Amherst conversation was on a less remote subject, and her admirable acquaintance with details enabled them to speak freely. Once she disputed a question concerning the Tottenham Hotspurs, and, obtaining silence by rapping a spoon, submitted it for decision to her father.

"My dear," he answered deferentially, "we don't want to talk shop. Not just yet awhile, at any rate."

His guests glanced meaningly at each other.

"Good gracious!" he cried, to a good-looking waiter with a large black moustache and a head of hair like a clothes brush, "what are you standing there gazing at me in such a melancholy way for?"

"Ver' sorry," said the young waiter.

"You look it!"

His nearest guests applauded the wit and readiness of the retort. Other tables cleared; folk hurried off to theatres. The head waiter ordered the moustached youth to turn off some of the lights.

"Now, gentlemen!" Mr. Amherst, leaning elbows on the table as coffee and liqueurs were served, cleared his throat, and sent a commanding glance up and down. "My dear" to his daughter, who was looking at the waiter "have I your attention?"

"Not yet, father."

"The presence of a lady," he said to the others, "need not interfere with the flow of conversation. I want you to make yourselves thoroughly at home, and do just as you please. We can wish each other a happy New Year later on in the evening. But first of all there's one small matter I wish to bring before your notice." They put hands to ears, in the attitude of men anxious to gain every word. He leaned back in his chair and came forward once more; his chin went out and he fired a name down the table. They twisted chairs promptly in his direction.

"Yes," gratified by their astonishment, "big game, I admit, but it's what I'm after. Other clubs may be on the same track, and therefore what we want first of all is absolute secrecy. If you're prepared to back me up I'll promise to see it through, but there must be no cackle, no chatterboxing, no talking to wives, or what not. Not a single word uttered away from this table."

"They won't let him go."

"Who said that?" The others, much in the manner of schoolboys, indicated Burnham.

"I believe," said Mr. Amherst "set me right if I'm wrong but I believe I'm Chairman. Unless I'm woefully mistaken, I was made Chairman about four years ago, at a time when the club was right out on the rocks. It had got a past, but no present. If my memory serves me right, I made it a small present. I bought shares when no one else was prepared to do so. And since that time, what has the club done?"

He put out the fingers of one hand and prepared to recite the successes. His daughter coughed.

"I was only going to run through the list, my dear."

"You can save yourself the trouble," she said.

"Now, having arrived at this point," addressing the table, "I ask myself the question, where are we weak? Where are we deficient? Where are we."

He was so much annoyed at their impatience in anticipating him by giving the answer, that he found himself obliged to apply a match to his cigar, which was still alight.

"Very well, then," reluctantly. "Discovering this, I look around and I endeavour to find out the best man available."

"Mr. Pangbourne," said Burnham, taking heart, "would no more think—"

Mr. Amherst snapped finger and thumb.

"That for Master Willie Pangbourne," he shouted. "No, no," irritably, to the moustached waiter, "I didn't call you. Go away and catch flies. I think, gentlemen," turning to the others, "that when I tell you I've known young Pangbourne since he was so high, and that not long ago I had to order him out of my house."

"Did he go?" asked the quiet voice at the other end.

"In point of fact he didn't go, Mary, my dear; but I distinctly ordered him to go. I don't mind a young man differing from me about politics, but there's a way of doing it. What I want to say is that Pangbourne isn't everybody. I can bring influence to bear on his directors. I've been accustomed to opposition all my life, and I'm not afraid of it. The only question is," he took a pear from the glass dish and shook it threateningly "how to raise the money."

The guests glanced at each other and became intent upon cigars. One or two wetted fingers and adjusted an unbroken leaf, thus escaping the inquiring look sent by Mr. Amherst.

"Tell you what," he cried, "I'll put down a trifle to make a start." He called to the waiter and said in a loud, distinct voice, "Onker." The other seemed puzzled, and the girl translated. The waiter brought ink, and on it being pointed out, somewhat bitterly, that this, by itself, was of little use, found pen and paper.

"There you are," said Mr. Amherst jovially. "Now pass it down this side and up the other. This is a tiled meeting, remember." He sat back and gazed at some cupids painted high up on the walls; the models apparently engaged after [they had dined at the restaurant. A nudge presently at his elbow told him the list had 'returned. He put on his pince-nez and inspected it. "Henry Amherst, 50," was the first item; the only other entry was in pencil, "Mary Amherst, threepence."

"And this," he said bitterly, "is, I suppose, what you call backing up the Chairman. Well, you're the best judges of your own actions. I never dictate to other people."

A murmur indicated doubt.

"Idea seems to be, sir," mentioned Burnham, "that we ought to leave well alone."

A few shy "Hear hears."

"We're very much obliged to you, Mr. Amherst, for your kind hospitality, and we've enjoyed meeting at your festive board if I may be allowed to use such an expression at this time of the year but you must understand we've none of us got money to throw away. We're devoted to footer, same as you are, and we've planked down as much as we could afford. We're pretty safe to cut a very fair figure this year, and—"

"Burnham," interrupted Mr. Amherst, "you'll excuse me, but perhaps you don't mind if I just say one syllable." He appeared to be under the impression that his voice had not hitherto been heard. "I've a great respect for you. You've got a shop in the borough that you've worked up from small beginnings, and, so far as I know, you've always paid your way."

"Come on," said Burnham desperately. "Let's hear what you are going to say on the other side."

"What I'm going to say on the other side is simply this. That, with all your estimable qualities, I've never, for a single, solitary moment, looked on you as anything but a fool."

"Father," reminded the girl, "these gentlemen are your guests."

"If you are so jolly keen on it," said Burnham, with spirit, "and if you particularly want to strengthen our team next season, why don't you put all the money down, and buy James McWinter for us?"

Mr. Amherst struck the table with the side of his large fist.

"Just," he declared emphatically, "just exactly what I intend to do."

The waiter came forward in the character of a hat-stand, and Mr. Amherst, grabbing at the nearest, found his irritation in no way lessened on discovering that it was headgear of insufficient size. Mary Amherst, turning to the waiter who stood now arms filled with overcoats, remarked pleasantly that a night like this must surely make him think of the clear blue skies and the dazzling sunshine of his native country; the waiter appeared to have acquired some of the useful idioms of the country, for he said in appealing undertones, "Half-time, half-time!" The head waiter came with the bill, which Mr. Amherst, in his annoyance, had forgotten. Miss Amherst was called upon to check the addition, and it became her duty to point out that the head waiter had by an excusable oversight in making a total reckoned the date at the top. This remedied, with profuse apologies, the party was conducted to the doorway.

"Also I don't mind telling you," said her father, speaking outside as though no interval had occurred since his last decisive remark, "exactly how much I'm prepared to go up to." He named a figure. "Not a farthing more," he declared resolutely. "What's that, my dear?"

"Only saying, father, that I was quite sure you couldn't afford it."

"That is my business, Mary."

"It was the business I was thinking about."

Mr. Amherst, never one to allow pasture land to flourish extensively under his boots, wrote a letter that night, posted it at the corner of Trafalgar Square, and walked three times around the pedestal of the Nelson Statue, partly because he had a great belief in the value of exercise, partly to enjoy the thought that he had, in sending the note, started the ball a-rolling. Coming into the hotel he was told by the porter that Miss Amherst had retired to rest, and he went upstairs humming cheerfully. The porter, it would seem, had been misinformed, for later the girl was leaning over the low balcony chatting with a youth who carried a kit bag. You would have said he was the young waiter at the Soho Restaurant, only that he wore no moustache and she called him Willie, which, as one knows, is rarely counted an Italian name.

"It's all right, dear girl," he said. "Now that I know his limit, I can easily arrange."

"I don't want him to waste his money," she explained.

"Leave everything to me," he begged. "Don't forget the match to-morrow. By the by, just go in and borrow a lucifer for me. My box is empty."

She returned with a supply taken from the smoking-room, and leaning over the balcony struck one and just managed to reach his cigar. No one was about, excepting the driver of a four-wheeler on the rank opposite; the cabman remarked confidentially to his horse: "Romeo and Juliet. Played nightly all over the blooming world." The horse waggled his nose-bag to show that he, too, was acquainted with standard literature.

Mr. Amherst had announced the intention of taking his daughter home by the eight thirty the following morning, and she was to knock at the wall not later than half-past seven; Miss Amherst was able at nine o'clock breakfast to exhibit her watch and blame it for her omission. She read from a morning paper the fixtures of the day, repeating the announcement concerning the match, whereupon her father announced that he was as ready to be hanged for a sheep as for a lamb, and gave her permission to catch the ten-five, and to travel alone. Miss Amherst agreed, but finding in another part of the journal an account of a deplorable case of a communication cord refusing to act, became suddenly terrified and begged her father to accompany her. He said "No!" There was reason in all things. Devoted as he was to his daughter, and ready as he might be to make sacrifices, this was asking too much. He had decided to see James Me Winter play once more, before advancing a further stage in the negotiations, and the opportunity was one not to be missed.

"But I tell you what, Mary," he said firmly; "you do some shopping, buy presents for relatives, and we can both go back together this evening."

"The best places in London close on Saturday afternoons."

"Then come to the match with me."

"I suppose I'd better," she said.

In London you see no such spectacle as can be witnessed in Midland and Northern towns, with the entire male population walking solidly in one direction, returning later in less regular order, and excited or depressed according to the fate of the home team. All the same, the compartments of the suburban train were well filled, and Mr. Amherst, fearful of being delayed, shouted on the crowded platform an instruction to his daughter.

"Look after yourself!"

An instruction she complied with the more readily because a hand waved to her from a carriage next to the engine. Half a dozen young men sprang up and offered places; she thanked them, and, apparently anxious not to be accused of favouritism, decided to hold by the rack and talk to young Pangbourne. As the train took a curve he had to hold her by the arm, but this she did not seem to mind. Pangbourne's directors were, of course, to be present at the game. A hurried conference had taken place that morning in the waiting-room of a London terminal station, and the price of James Me Winter, on Mr. Pangbourne's urgent suggestion, had been fixed at a price that far exceeded the limit mentioned by Miss Amherst's father.

"That's capital!" she declared gratefully "capital in more senses than one. You see, Willie, I can remember the time when we were hard up at home, and I recollect how my mother had to scheme and contrive. I don't want to find myself going back. And the sum represents such an awful lot of money. Football's a good sport, but there are other games."

"Marriage, for instance?"

"We can talk of that," she said composedly, "later on. Let's settle one matter first. We mustn't be seen talking to each other, mind."

Mr. Amherst apologised to his daughter, as they made their way to the entrance to the ground, for his apparent neglect, and she accepted his excuses so readily that he felt bound to point out that, in a general way, he did look after her very carefully, adding that there was no one else to do this. Everything, said Mr. Amherst, with a touch of importance and a hint at real affection, devolved upon him, and he was not the man to flinch responsibilities. She inquired, deferentially, whether he considered it wise to pay out such a large sum of money for James Me Winter. He replied that James was worth the figure mentioned the previous night, but not a penny, not a halfpenny more. If the other club began to haggle and bargain and huckster, he, Mr. Amherst, would instantly withdraw.

"And what I say," he declared, "as you very well know, is what I stick to. My first word is my last word. Is that so, my dear, or isn't it?"

"You're an extraordinary man, father." He appeared content with this vague admission.

Quite a good number had taken advantage of the hospitable offer to ladies, and Mr. Amherst, in spite of his recent declaration, showed relief on encountering the wife of another director, willing and ready to take charge of his daughter. Silk hat at back of head, he hurried off. "Highly important business!" he explained. Mrs. Burnham, a matronly person, confessed that she knew nothing and cared nothing for the game, but had to affect an interest in order to make opportunity of keeping an eye on her husband. Husbands required a lot of watching. Husbands were kittle cattle, if the truth was known. Husbands being what they were, the wonder was that any married lady remained in possession of her senses; she herself foresaw clearly the time when she would be taken away to the County Asylum. Having said all this, and having mentioned that she counted herself among the few who could respect and keep a secret, Mrs. Burnham lowered her voice that folk around might not hear, and urged it was high time Miss Amherst thought of getting married. Mrs. Burnham 's advice was that Miss Amherst should pick out some desirable young gentleman of good birth and excellent prospects.

"And then go for him," recommended the matronly lady, with earnestness. "Go for him, for all you know. Takes a bit of doing, of course, but it's worthwhile."

The commencement of the game did not interrupt Mrs. Burnham 's counsel, but it interfered with the girl's power of giving attention. Standing on a chair she watched eagerly, describing the progress in brief ejaculatory sentences to her chaperon; joined in the appeals of a few members of the crowd addressed to the visiting team; refrained from giving assistance to the majority in cheering and encouraging the home side. Privately, she criticised James Me Winter, who, a large young man, appeared to be doing as little as possible, the while the rest scurried about on the slightly frosted turfed ground, doing everything in a strenuous manner with no result. What a football crowd likes is the scoring of goals, and when at half-time it proved that not one had been recorded on either side, the two teams, exhausted and limp (with the exception of James Me Winter) were followed by regretful looks; men described what they themselves would have done, if they were but a few years younger or older, and less occupied with other affairs. Mr. Amherst bustled around, fanning himself with his silk hat, and looking greatly perturbed. He mentioned to his daughter that they (meaning Pangbourne's directors) had the cheek to ask so much quoting the large figure that he would see them further before planking down that amount; he went so far as to hint at the well-warmed direction they could select. The teams took up their new positions. The whistle sounded. Before Miss Amherst had disengaged herself from her companion's inquiries and counsel, the outside left, amidst erroneous cries of "Off-side!" centred across to the inside right, who centred again, and James McWinter trapped the ball, dodged the two backs and shot hard; the goalkeeper fumbled it, and even supporters of the home side could scarce restrain a cheer. The other team prepared for a change of tactics, and in exactly four minutes precisely the same thing happened, and the goalkeeper dealt with the ball in almost the same manner; tears stood in his eyes; he glanced with reproach at his gloves, and bowed his head penitently to the observations of colleagues. Miss Amherst had to apologise more than once when crying "Shoot!" for kicking the back of a stout gentleman standing just in front of her. When at the end of the ninety minutes' traffic the visiting side had scored five to none, and four of these goals were to be credited to James McWinter, she turned to her companion. Her father was in a kind of scrum not far off; she recognised the light in his eyes of one to whom money was of no consequence, and into her eyes came the light of one resolved to act promptly. Under cover of the cheering, she made an enthusiastic and apparently genuine declaration.

"Oh, but, my dear," cried Mrs. Burnham alarmedly, "you mustn't talk like this. This is dreadful. When I said what I did just now, I never meant you should go and throw yourself away on a great clumsy hulk like that, earning not more than 4 a week. Besides, his people are meat salesmen."

"I'm not a vegetarian."

Mr. Amherst, scarlet, almost blue with eagerness, was hurrying by.

"Not a word, please," begged the girl, with extravagant signs of distress, "not a syllable to my father. Promise me you won't tell him. My mind's made up; but I don't want him to know."

Mrs. Burnham put out the hooked handle of her umbrella and caught Mr. Amherst neatly. "Very sorry," he panted, "can't spare a moment."

"You just come here first," ordered the lady resolutely. "There's something you've got to know, and I mean to tell it to you before I go and look after my husband. I'm not going to be blamed afterwards, and have you say it was my fault."

"Do hurry up," begged Mr. Amherst piteously. "If you knew how urgent it all was, you wouldn't chatter on like this. I'm going to give them whatever they ask for him. He's a bachelor, and he won't mind where he lives."

"Your daughter," said Mrs. Burnham, speaking with tragic emphasis, "tells me that she's fallen in love at first sight with that six foot three called James McSomething who's been kicking the ball like a young demon between the two posts. And my advice to you is keep 'em well apart keep 'em hundreds of miles apart from each other!"

Mr. Pangbourne's club, with the aid of James and the rest, made its way later into the Second League, and he himself secured three well-paid official appointments from the Corporation and other bodies, who were probably actuated by feelings of gratitude; the entire town joined in giving him and Miss Amherst a notable wedding present. Mr. Amherst, now honorary secretary of the Bowling Club, has married a lady of forty-five, hitherto interested only in deep-sea fishermen. And all intend to live more or less happily ever afterwards.

VII

A CASE OF SUSPICION

It was pleasant to get about the square of the station where luggage had to be labelled and heated passengers stormed at porters and a rather stout brass bell was rung, and where at moments of pressure it did seem that the world had suddenly gone mad pleasant to stroll there and to feel you were one of the few who recognised the identity of the quiet man smoking a briar pipe and carrying an umbrella, over near the label case. He was middle-aged, with an unobtrusive manner; in the summer he wore a straw hat sedately; he seemed to be always waiting for a train that never arrived. If a loiterer made his way into the station and stood about the bookstall longer than seemed necessary, the quiet man would go near to him, moving when he moved, stopping when he stopped, and losing no sight of him until he went off. The quiet man had apparently no friends, and the staff addressed him rarely.

Now the Station Master's boy knew that this man was a retired member of the police force, the plain-clothes detective attached to the terminus. And in connection with a predecessor of this mysterious official they told him, in the Up Parcels Office, an incident.

Sergeant Bellchambers had not succeeded in gaining the popularity that most men, in this world, desire, but one or two of his first investigations received favourable comment from the General Manager, and this repaid him for lack of sympathy from others. It was said that in the M. division they had been glad to see him take his pension and go, the opinion of the Inspector's desk being that Bell-chambers was a born muddler. This might have been the invention of the station staff; what was quite certain was that in his reports on blue paper in the early cases referred to he fixed blame on men whom the station considered innocent, and these men were, in consequence, fined or reduced. Moreover, he had not been content with singling out individuals and recommending them for the stocks, but he condemned an entire department; for which reason the station said darkly:

"We shall 'ave to get our own back." This was the state of things when the cigar robberies began. Parcels of cigars came up regularly from a certain firm and from a certain local station, sometimes for delivery in London, sometimes for transfer to another railway; one parcel in four reached its destination in good appearance outwardly, but with part of the contents abstracted. The firm made heavy claims, wrote furious letters, and at last managed to get a communication into the public press in which bitter reference was made to the supineness and slothful behaviour of the railway company. The Superintendent of the Line sent for Bellchambers, withdrawing him from easy duties on the station square.

"The only question is," said the high official.

"Where do these robberies take place?" suggested Bellchambers. "That's the point," he added sagely, "that's what we've got to get at."

"What is your opinion, Sergeant?"

Sergeant Bellchambers made a fine pretence of taking thought before he answered. Then with red-ink pen he wrote on an envelope and passed it across the table.

"Up Office," read the Superintendent.

"'Ush," said Bellchambers warningly.

"Do you think you can find the thieves?"

"If I'm given a free hand," said Bellchambers, "and no quibble raised, sir, about my petty disbursements."

"Go in and win," said the Superintendent. "When do you start?"

"This very night, sir?"

"Let me have a report in the morning."

That evening the head of the department sent to the Up Office a new hand to assist the late-duty men. He was black-bearded with a very ruddy face, and he wore a uniform that had apparently belonged to a shorter and a slimmer person. His name, he said, was Edward Jones, but the Up Office seemed not contented with this and decided on the suggestion of a junior clerk to call him by the title of "Sunset." He settled to the work with moderate determination, calling off parcels and sorting them into bins for delivery with perhaps more intelligence than the raw amateur usually showed: he spoke in a hoarse voice, and this he accounted for by confessing himself a slave to tobacco; he discussed the matter with the other men, between the arrival of trains, and seemed, not unnaturally, more interested in those who smoked than in the one or two who limited themselves to a cigarette a week, consumed after dinner on Sundays. The Up Office always had a composite scent, in which fruit, game, cheese, and other things mixed, with sometimes one gaining ascendancy, sometimes another; a new flavour of a more pleasant and a vaguer character was contributed presently by a small brown-paper covered box, brought in from an arrival platform, bearing a proud label:

VALUABLE CIGARS. KEEP DRY.

"'Ere's a chance for some one," said the porter, as he called it off. "Sunset, old chum, these'd do your palate good."

"Silly thing to mark 'em like that," remarked the new man. "It's throwing temptation in anybody's way. I should say they're likely enough worth about fifteen pence to one-and-six a-piece."

"How d' you know?"

"I don't profess to know," said the new man hurriedly. "I'm only giving a rough estimate. But bless my soul," he went on after a pause, "what a refining influence a cigar has."

"If it's a good one," suggested a boy porter.

"They're all good," declared the new man with enthusiasm. "They're like the ladies in that respect. Some are better 'n others, but they're all good."

"Not a married man, then?" asked a foreman.

"I'm a bloomin' bachelor," said the new chum. "And what a thing it is on your Sunday off, when you're waiting at the end of her road, to light up a cigar with a fine aroma to it. It not only gives you an air of belonging to the 'igher aristocracy, but it also carries away any suspicion of corduroy that might be 'anging about."

"I've never give less than twopence," remarked the boy porter.

"I'm sorry for you," said the new man. "I should have thought a chap with your fore'ead had got more ambition. Why, when I was a lad of your height—"

"Pardon me," interrupted the foreman, "you seem to 'ave a most extraordinary flow of conversation."

"I'm celebrated for it."

"I wonder," said the foreman curiously, "whether you'd mind stopping it for a moment and doing a bit of work instead. Reason I suggest it is that the Company pays you for what you do and not for what you talk."

"I can take a 'int," said the new man coldly.

There seemed a desire on the part of the others that night to make Porter Jones work as hard as it is possible for a man to work. The heaviest hampers were confided to his care; the slimiest cases of fish were placed upon his shoulder; he it was who was told off to see to some consignments of rather advanced venison. The parcel of valuable cigars remained in the Number Five bin to be transferred to another Company by the first delivery in the morning, and it was observed that whenever Porter Jones came into the office he glanced in that direction. Now the Up Office, as I have hinted, had been perturbed over the recent complaints, and the mere fact that they had to fill up memoranda in regard to the various investigations, to the effect that, "I beg to say in reference to the attached papers that I know nothing whatever of the matter, I am, sir, your obedient servant," this in itself was enough to put a keener edge on observation. Wherefore, a secret meeting was held near the gas-stove by the booking-up desk, and it was decided that the new man should be watched closely; it was felt it would be a proud and estimable thing for the office, the character of which was at this period slurred, if it could itself detect a wrong-doer and take him to justice. And should it happen that the detected one proved to be a new man with no friends in the department to lament his fall, then the most doubtful would have to revert to old beliefs in a wise and thoughtful Providence. Their suspicions were increased by the fact that whenever Porter Jones, in the brief intervals between work from nine o'clock onwards, resumed conversation, he invariably bent its direction towards the subject of cigars.

"Take no notice," whispered the foreman to his colleagues. "At least when I say take no notice, I mean take all the notice you can, but keep your little heads shut as tight as possible."

"Shall one of us lay up for him?"

"Who's the smallest?" asked the foreman, with an air of having already thought of this device.

"I are," said the boy porter.

"Evidently," remarked the foreman, looking down at him, "evidently a chap of superior education. Country born, ain't you?"

"I were."

"Then," said the foreman, "up you jump behind them 'books off' and you watch, my lad, watch Sunset for all you are worth."

The Up Office closed at midnight in order to sleep for a few hours. Before that time the men had made preparations for departure, packing shining hand-bags and exchanging the official cap for a bowler hat, and brushing their boots; this last act is one of which the railway man never tires. Porter Jones alone seemed to be taking no preliminary steps, and when asked where he lived replied lightly and evasively that he should probably finish up at the Carlton Club. The gas lights were turned down one by one and darkness increased its possession of the office. Porter Jones went up to the end where Bin Number Five was situated; the others hummed to give a suggestion of unconcern. Suddenly there was commotion at the darkened end of the office, and seizing hand lamps, they hurried forward.

"Old him, 'old him," cried the boy porter. The counsel seemed unnecessary, for he gripped Porter Jones most effectively by the collar of the corduroy jacket. "Set on his 'ead. Lam him one."

"What's all this fuss about?" demanded the foreman.

"He's got it," screamed the boy porter. "Sunset's got it hid under his jacket."

"Got what hid?" asked the foreman. "Let's 'ave the facts first of all."

"I can easily explain," gasped the new man. "I only wanted to see if—Make him leave go. He's—he's throttling me."

"He's a-trying to," admitted the boy porter.

"Let him loose," ordered the foreman. "Men, stand around him so as he can't make his escape. What's that bulging under your arm, matey?"

The new man gave an awkward laugh, as he withdrew the labelled parcel.

"I can explain it all to you," he said, addressing the foreman and trying to rebutton his torn collar, "if you will favour me with two minutes alone outside."

"Don't you do it," advised the others. "See him 'anged first."

"Whatsoever you 'ave to say," declared the foreman steadily, "you'd better say it here and now."

"Well, it's like this. I'm the detective."

"Ho!" said the foreman satirically. "Detective and thief in one, eh? Vurry 'appy combination, I must say."

"See here," said the other, annoyed at the incredulous tone, "I'll take off this beard and then you can some of you identify me."

As he did so the foreman held up his hand lamp, examining the features carefully.

"Do any of you chaps recognise him?"

The staff replied at once that to the best of their belief they had never before in this world set eyes on him.

"Don't play the goat," he urged anxiously. "We've all got our duties to perform."

"That's true; we shall 'ave to lock you up for the night."

"Right you are," said the other gleefully. "Take me round to the nearest police station and then—"

"That would mean losing our last train 'ome," pointed out the foreman.

"I s'pose," said the boy porter respectfully, "it wouldn't do to put him in the lamp room?"

"Chaps," said the foreman, "my idea is we'd better, I think, put him in the lamp room. Get Porter Swan to lend you the keys, my lad. As for you, you scoundrel."

"If you so much as dare to lock me up there I'll see that you regret it every day of your lives." He argued vehemently.

"Look 'ere, me man," said the boy porter, returning with the keys, "we want none of your empty threats. If you think we're going to be bluffed by a chap of your caliber."

"My what?" shouted the indignant man, struggling to get at the lad.

"Go on, my child," said the foreman approvingly. "Let him have some of your long ones." The foreman turned to the others.

"This is where your school teaching comes in 'andy," he whispered.

"A chap of your caliber," repeated the boy porter, encouraged; "you're labouring under the very worst misapprehension."

"Good!" said the others. "Worst misapprehension that you ever suffered from or endured or tolerated or submitted to or underwent or—"

"That's enough for him," interrupted the foreman, "we'd best not overdo it. Got his arms tied, lads?"

"You'll suffer for this," he cried.

"I'll take me oath you will," said the foreman. "Now then, two of you at each arm and march! Boy, blow out the gas and lock up."

No one was encountered on the way to the lamp room who had authority to interfere with the plans of the Up Office, and the unfortunate man was conducted at a sharp walk to that gloomy, sooty, greasy haven. The place reeked with oily waste, and some appeared to have been smouldering, giving a result that nice people would call displeasing. The uneven flooring was laid out with lakes of dirty water; zinc counters did not permit themselves to be touched. The foreman turned out the one glimmer of light as though by accident.

"Got a match on you?" he asked the prisoner in a kindly tone.

"Only one box."

"Hand it over", ordered the foreman, "for a moment. Thanks," slipping it into his pocket. "Now we can catch our twelve fifteen. Good night, old sort."

"'Appy dreams," cried the others.

"Don't be late in the morning," called out the boy porter.

The imprisoned man, not daring to trust himself to reply, heard the door close, heard the lock shoot. He groaned, and began to reckon the black hours that he would have to endure in the place; at the least, the number would be six; he did not care to think what it might be at the most. Throughout the 'whole of the time he was unable to close his eyes, and his only relief to the length of the hours came by thinking of the report that he would indite the following morning. He polished up in his mind some of the references to the boy porter, and to the man who gripped his arm in bringing him from the Up Office; it seemed that his suspicions in regard to the pilferages were centred, for some reason, on those who had most aggrieved him. Before daylight began to grin at him through the barred window of the lamp room he had mentally completed his report, and the last paragraph he felt was especially good.

"I am able to speak with absolute certainty, and I can go so far as to say the men who are undoubtedly responsible for the recent pilferages are those I have named, and I beg to suggest respectfully that steps be taken to relieve them of their present duties at the earliest possible moment. The only alternative is a clean sweep of the whole of the Up Office staff, and this, sir, I hesitate to recommend. But for reasons that I have stated, and for others which I think it wise not to place upon paper, I earnestly hope that the recommendation I have made will be acted upon without delay.

"W. BELLCHAMBERS.

"P.S. Especially the foreman and the junior."

"Can't make it hotter for them," said Sergeant Bellchambers to himself regretfully, "without it looking as though I'd got some personal spite."

The night seemed endless, but it proved to have a finish, and Bellchambers, when the lamp-man opened the door in the morning, went out, a tired, oil-scented, yawning, but a determined official. A wash and a shave increased the last quality, and when the Superintendent arrived at nine o'clock, morning paper under his arm, Sergeant Bellchambers was waiting for him in the lobby of the office with confidence written all over his face in large letters.

"Evening, sir."

"Good-morning, Sergeant."

"I mean morning," corrected Bellchambers. "I've been up all night over that little affair you spoke about."

"Ah!" said the Superintendent, sitting down in his arm-chair, "with no result?"

"On the contrary, sir," said Sergeant Bellchambers importantly. "If it isn't troubling you too much I'll trouble you to cast your eyes over this report of mine."

The Superintendent let his glasses flick open and adjusted them on his nose. The Sergeant, leaning one arm on the mantelpiece, watched his superior officer, waiting for the sign of gratified approval. This, to his great astonishment, did not come, and the Superintendent's face remained unchanged when he had thrown the report on the shining table.

"Do you mean to say that you want me to get rid of these men?"

"That was the impression," said the Sergeant, with a touch of acidity, "I intended to convey."

"And you think they're guilty?"

"I'll stake my reputation on it, sir," said Sergeant Bellchambers.

"That is not much of a bet," remarked the other.

"You can take it from me that these pilferages will never cease until the men I've referred to are turned out."

"I'm very anxious to do something," said the Superintendent, taking up a ruler thoughtfully.

"Like myself, sir," said Bellchambers. "That's me all over."

"But not," said the Superintendent, hitting the table, "not in the direction you suggest. Head this!"

He handed over the morning paper to Sergeant Bellchambers, pointing to a letter headed "Recent Complaints of Pilferages."

"Ah!" said the Sergeant exultingly, "they're going for us again, then. "Dear Sir," he read. "With reference to our letters to you complaining of abstraction from our parcels of cigars sent by railway, we think it only right to inform you that we have discovered these pilferages were made by one of our own men. It appears that after delivering the parcels at the station here, and after they were weighed, he was in the habit of offering to take them to the train, and whilst doing this effected the robberies to which reference has been made. We need scarcely point out that if the station had been wisely managed these lamentable occurrences would in all probability never have taken place; the only question is, who is responsible? We are, dear sir, yours faithfully."

"A paltry trick to play on anybody," said the Sergeant. "At the same time, sir, I think there'll be no harm in making a change in the staff."

"I intend to do so. Will you keep your eyes open, Sergeant."

"Ain't they always?"

"And," said the Superintendent, "look out for another berth. Shut the door quietly after you."

VIII

QUESTION OF TEMPERATURE

L.O.M. caught sight of M.R. two or three times on the journey, and M.R. made more than one effort to obtain completer details by inspection of the blue card label on L.O.M.'s bag. A certain coolness on M.R's side marked their first meeting, but this was the fault of the English Channel; it certainly looked like a practical joke, not quite in good taste, when a sudden lurch of the steamer gent him against her on the upper deck; despite his apologies, there was about the incident a suggestion of Holloway Road on Sunday evenings. M.R. told her married sister that she considered him a bounder; the married sister replied that this description could be applied to men in general, with one single exception. "Be very careful, Margaret," she added, "how you make acquaintances. We shall run up against all sorts."

"All sorts," complained the girl, "seem to be running up against me."

At the Paris Station of the Lyons railway, L.O.M. appeared in a more favourable light, rescuing the married sister's coat which had been taken from a peg in the buffet by a Frenchwoman who was either short-sighted or deficient in honesty. At Vallorbes, it was he who came to the window of their compartment the hour being five a.m., and snow on the ground and gave the welcome news that their registered luggage was not amongst the packages selected for examination at the Swiss frontier.

"Do you think I might get you some coffee?" he asked.

"Certainly not!" answered the married sister promptly.

The incident constituted a subject for discussion, the younger girl contending that the obliging male should never be curtly repulsed; the other arguing that a difficulty would have been found in persuading the youth to accept cash for refreshments supplied, and, consequent on this, the trouble in preventing him from becoming intrusive could scarcely be measured. At Lausanne, where passengers took breakfast, he very properly kept his distance. At Bex, in the tram-cars, which were to make the climb with the aid of motive power at the back, he gave up his place to the elder of the two and sat side by side with the girl in the crowded luggage van.

"Yes," she replied, "I skate, and I should like to learn to ski. Do you?"

"Moderately good at it," replied L.O.M. "Did some in Norway."

"Then, perhaps—"

"You will find an instructor up there," he said.

She turned away huffily.

It was not, however, easy to avoid joining in the general conversation. Everybody had projects for the filling up of the winter holiday; the conductor, as the car went slowly up the hill, was appealed to for information concerning weather, and being a man of cheerful temperament, gave exactly the particulars that were hoped and desired, without allowing truth to mar the effect. Thus an atmosphere of hopefulness pervaded the luggage van, and even retiring military men perched upon trunks became vivacious, talking of desperate deeds already accomplished in other places on toboggans, and speaking with relish of the appetite that came after these exercises. The two were soon again in conversation, and the girl mentioned that her sister's maiden name was Rodgers, a fact which enabled him to perceive acutely that this must be also the girl's name. Turning the label on his valise, he introduced himself.

"Masterson," he said.

"I like names of three syllables," she remarked.

The hour and a half occupied by the journey was lessened by all this, and by the increasingly snowy aspect of the mountains on either side of the track; the conductor derided this as trifling, and endeavoured to give some idea of the downfall that had taken place up near the summit. At Gryon the steep part finished, and the cars went on with the assistance of overhead wires.

"You play and sing, I suppose?"

"I perform no parlour tricks of any description," said Miss Rodgers definitely. "I leave these accomplishments to others."

"Really?" Rather taken back, and the movement of his forehead slightly lifting his cap. "I had an idea I'd got the notion that every girl did. My sisters—"

"I am the exception" with pride. "Outdoor sports constitute my strong point. I could live forever in the open air."

"What about the bad weather?" inquired Masterson.

"How can you talk of bad weather at a time like this? Look back and see that dear, white, delightful little village. Tell me, do you think there will be a carnival on the ice rink? I've brought the sweetest fancy dress you ever saw. You won't find me staying indoors, excepting for meals."

When the cars reached the destination, the two alone out of the whole party exhibited scarcely any signs of the twenty-five hours' journey from Charing Cross and London; the married sister compensated by showing every symptom of collapse, and he very courteously assisted her up the wooden steps and over the bridge to the hotel. There the flurried manager checked names as they entered; assigned the double room on the first floor to Mr. Masterson, and the single room on the third floor to Miss Rodgers and her exhausted sister; they united forces in protesting against this, and became more friendly in the presence of a common grievance. Despite the warmth of arguments used by visitors, the thermometer near the pile of brushes and toboggans registered four degrees of frost.

Lunch was served at once, and immediately after the meal the married sister, discovering that she had eaten veal under the impression it was mutton, announced her intention of resting indoors during the afternoon. The other two came down in jerseys and white caps, and the married sister gave Masterson gracious permission to escort Miss Rodgers to the rink.

"Mind you bring her back safely," she commanded.

"I'll do my best," he said.

"Quite capable of taking care of myself," remarked the girl. "Just lace up my boots for me, please." They left the lady in the vestibule perusing a Cardiff journal bearing date of a Tuesday in the previous month.

One could see on their return that the afternoon on the rink had reached highest expectations; their animation caused some compression of the eyebrows on the part of sedater folk taking tea. Everything had happened as the flushed, excited girl wanted it to happen. Her ability had excited favourable comment from other skaters; one of the professionals gave a compliment; the band played delightfully, and she not caring for indoor dancing completely and thoroughly enjoyed a waltz. Sun shining all the time.

"After tea," she explained, "we are going out to do some skiing."

"Who is meant, pray," asked her sister carefully, "by the word 'we'?"

"Mr. Masterson and myself, of course!"

"Oh!" commented her sister, giving an inflection which the printed word cannot convey.

"What's your objection, Ellen?"

"It would be useless for me to offer any. I shall stay in and write. Does he know that you neither play nor sing?"

"I've told him," snapped the girl.

Folk at the hotel attended meals with regularity, but their impatience towards the finish was something not easily concealed. A tall woman seated opposite at dinner, and possessing a complexion which looked almost natural, hinted that she was arranging some amateur theatricals, and Mr. Masterson gave to the announcement an interest which Miss Rodgers considered so excessive that she turned from him and listened with attention intended to be equally extravagant to her sister's talk concerning Henry. The lady with the complexion had been searching the hotels for some one who could sing and act; up to the present, she had found three able to sing, but not greatly desirous of doing so; they were more definite in their replies to her invitation in regard to acting. Also, she required some one who could play the piano-forte readily.

"Please help me if you can," she begged, passing the French mustard across to Mr. Masterson, and assuming an ingratiating smile. "I shall be so grateful."

"There's a good deal to do out-of-doors," he mentioned.

"Then," said the lady, with resolution, "I must pray for mild weather!"

The concierge announced in the vestibule, as folk returned who had been out for moonlight tobogganing after dinner, that the frost was hard, the thermometer promising well; bridge players ordered him to close the doors, and keep them closed, but Masterson and Miss Rodgers coming in, flushed with exercise on the snow run, congratulated each other on the good news, and in the corridor, before saying good-night, made full and complete plans for the following day.

Masterson slept the sleep of a well-tired man until six o'clock, when the bell rang to arouse servants. He heard a drip, drip, drip from the roofs, and turning over dreamt of an amazing leap on skis from the top of Mont Blanc to the Dent du Midi, an exploit that created in his mind, not surprise, but genuine satisfaction. When he awoke again, it was to find the hour late, and in dressing hastily, to avoid the fifty centimes fine inflicted on those who took breakfast after ten, he shared the blame between himself and the heating apparatus which kept the room at a too comfortable temperature.

"Really very sorry," he cried, entering the dining-room. Severe faces looked up from the tables; young Miss Rodgers helped her sister to honey and sighed. "You can't think how full of regret I am."

"It is a pity," she said.

"I was awake early, mind you," he went on eagerly. "Wide awake as I am now. And then I dozed off, and when I—"

The waiting maid brought his coffee and he poured it into the cup with the air of a man not deserving refreshment.

"You have been out alone, I suppose?" he remarked.

"Apparently," interposed the married sister, "you are not aware that there has been a most wonderful thaw during the night, and that there is now a thick mist."

The weather was not the only thing affected by the change. After breakfast, folk stood about in the corridor examining the notices there with a doleful expression. "Rink Closed" stood out in definite capital letters, and eyes turned from the stern announcement to gain some comfort from the slips which recorded loss of decorative articles. A few proclaimed intention of devoting the morning to sending postcards, and to the clearing off of arrears in correspondence, and stalked resolutely up to the drawing-room; others went to see if they could induce the concierge to make a cheerful prophecy concerning the weather, returning with the news that the official, discouraged by failure, refused to hold out anything that looked like hope. One or two inspected time tables and talked of going back to Lausanne.

"Why don't you suggest something, Mr. Masterson?"

"Wish I had the necessary intelligence, Miss Rodgers. Is there anything we can arrange indoors, I wonder, to make the time go quickly whilst the weather is sorting itself? Think of something that you're good at!"

"If you possessed a memory," retorted the girl warmly, "you would recollect that I distinctly told you."

The lady with the very fresh complexion interposed, with an apology. Would Mr. Masterson give her three minutes of his time in a corner of the vestibule? Masterson looked at the girl for directions, but she turned away, and he followed the other obediently.

Great mystery surrounded the ball-room, and especially the stage of the ball-room, that day, with janitors at doors, asking those who arrived: "Excuse me, but are you taking part?" and when a negative answer was given, adding: "Then will you kindly stay outside, please?" The pianoforte could be heard being played with the soft pedal down r and a sound came of choruses; occasionally the voice of the made-up lady crying: "Oh, that's not a bit like it!" and "We must try the first act all over again!" and "Do take up your cues smartly, please!"

At lunch she escorted Masterson into the dining-room, conveying him past the chairs occupied by Miss Rodgers and the married sister, and induced him to sit beside her during the meal. The doyen of the guests rapped three times on the table between the veal and the chicken course, and made an announcement. Volunteers were required to sing in the church choir. A bracelet had been found on the billiard table. To-morrow evening there would be a theatrical entertainment in the ball-room under the joint superintendence of Miss Ellicott and Mr. Masterson. Ladies willing to sing in the chorus were requested to communicate immediately with Mr. Masterson. The doyen sat down; the buzz of conversation recommenced.

Masterson, note-book in hand, stood at the doorway when the meal was over, taking names. As Miss Rodgers and her sister came near, he looked up inquiringly, but the girl stared at him in a distant manner, and went past, ignoring the half-completed question which he put to her; Masterson gazed after them with the abashed look of one who has discovered that he does not fully understand women, and to the next offer replied, rather brusquely, that the list was now complete. He proceeded to the ball-room and gave up the afternoon to rehearsal, interspersed with gusty arguments with the leading lady. Outside, the rain came down in a quiet, orderly manner, as though it were doing exactly what was required, and the concierge went about assuring visitors that the fault was not his.

Young Miss Rodgers, wearing defiance as a cloak to nervousness, knocked at the door of the ball-room and asked to see Mr. Masterson. The amateur door-keeper replied that the gentleman was busy. Miss Rodgers, with a smile that would have persuaded even a professional, induced the door-keeper to go and make further inquiries, and immediately that he had started on this errand, not only slipped inside the room, but at once slipped up on the polished floor. Now, she was a sure-footed girl, not accustomed to tumble, and it was fortunate, in view of her record, that no one happened to witness the incident. She had resumed an upright position when the doorkeeper returned.

"You go across to the drawing-room," he whispered importantly, "and in about ten minutes he'll see you! Quarter of an hour at the outside."

The entire strength of the company was on the stage, and as she walked up and down the carpeted room, snatches of the dialogue came to her ears. The leading lady and Masterson were about to go through once again the scene which had startled the girl on entering the ball-room; the lady suggested improvements. "When I rush into your arms," she said, "how would it be for you to catch me like this," here evidently followed an illustration "and I'll lean my hand on your shoulder like this" another illustration "and then we can start the duet." Masterman's voice said he was ready to try this plan. "That's better," remarked the lady presently, "but I think we may as well do it again. Give me the word, somebody."

The girl peered through the cracks of the set scenery on the stage, and, her hand at her throat, watched and listened.

"That's about right. Now for the duet. Play the symphony, please, Miss Jenner." After this, "Thank you. Just once more."

Masterson's voice, a strong baritone, started:

"As I look into eyes that gaze up into mine, I know that your dear heart is beating for me. I know you're as true as the stars that do shine, As the sun and the moon and the earth and the sea. Yet I ask for one word."

Miss Rodgers, fearful of being discovered and unable to endure contemplation of the scene any longer, crept away to the other end of the drawing-room, where, regarding herself in the mirror, she found an extremely cross looking face with a line or two on the forehead. As the lady's reply rang out, the girl took up an illustrated journal from the table and endeavoured to divert her thoughts by concentrating on fashion, only to find that she could not be quite sure whether she was inspecting a page of drawings or a page of letterpress.

"For I love thee, I love thee, 'tis all I can say."

The chorus, standing around with a strange want of delicacy during this affectionate argument, now threw off all restraint, and acknowledged the interest they had taken in the proceedings by singing confidentially to each other:

"She loves him, she loves him, 'tis all he can say,
He loves her, he loves for a year and a day.
Pray see how affection has come their direction,
Oh, thrice happy twain to be wedded in May."

"Hullo!" cried Masterson, astonished, coming off, "you here?"

The question seemed to be one of those not requiring a reply, and Miss Rodgers ignored it.

"I wanted to know whether there was a chance of being able to help," she said.

"Rather!" he declared readily. "We'll soon see about that. I'll go and arrange."

He went at a good rate; returned with leaden footsteps.

"I'm sorry!" she said, receiving his message.

"If you had only offered earlier," he remarked apologetically. "You see, I'm not in charge of the affair, or else I'd manage it like a shot. And I thought you said—"

"It occurred to me," explained Miss Rodgers, her voice faltering slightly, "that I'd like to try. But it doesn't really matter in the least."

Her sister was in a convalescent state, ready to talk of subjects other than Henry, and when the girl burst into the room which they jointly occupied, and throwing herself on the red couch, gave way to tears, comfort was close at hand. The sister wisely refrained at first from putting questions, allowed the girl to have her cry out, and only said soothingly, "It's all right, dearie. Don't worry more than you can help."

When composure returned, the solace of the confessional was utilised and the married sister listened, interjecting now and again, "Yes, I understand," and "I quite see what you mean."

"You don't mind, I hope, if I point out," she remarked, when the last word had been said, "that mother and I have always been persuading you to take up music or singing or some accomplishment of the kind."

"I know," admitted the girl penitently.

"And you have always said there were plenty of girls who could do these things, and that you were not going to bother about them. Now you see how important it is that you should keep them level with others. You must make hay whilst the sun shines," quoted the married sister.

"I shall have to make a start." "And when we get back to London, you are going to set to work at once and learn some of these useful accomplishments?"

"I promise," declared Miss Rodgers resolutely. "And I think, too, I should like to take up cooking. One never knows when it may come in handy."

The performance went well, and nothing could have exceeded the graciousness of young Miss Rodgers towards the leading lady; few of the later compliments exceeded hers. Indeed, when, on the following day, the frost returned succeeded by a pleasant sprinkling of snow, she offered to take the leading lady out on the rink and charge herself with the responsibility of teaching the art of skating.

"No, dear," replied the other. "Thank you very much, but no. As a matter of fact, although I try my best not to look it, I'm too old. Look after Mr. Masterson, instead. He admires you, and you mustn't lose any chance of persuading him to continue to do so, indoors or out. I know what men are!"

IX

FOREIGN AFFAIRS

We parted from Mr. Peter A. Chasemore at Bologna owing to a slight difference of opinion. Carolyn Stokes and myself had the notion that we should find Venice damp and possibly cold; Mr. Chasemore declared that to go home without seeing a gondola would give him a pain compared with which rheumatism might be considered a sensation of acute delight. There is no use denying the fact that we two women missed Mr. Chasemore a good deal. Confusion took place on the journey, for which I blamed Carolyn Stokes, and she blamed me. When with the assistance of luck we did reach the Belvedere our tempers were not improved by the fact that a young man and an elderly lady occupied, for the moment, the attention of the hotel people.

"Norman," she said to him, as the proprietor eventually came to us, "you can consider yourself free for the remainder of the day." He bowed. "Give me that; I will take charge of it." Both Carolyn Stokes and myself noticed the name on the label as the leather case was being transferred.

I suppose the fact that there are no such titles where we come from caused the encounter to make an impression upon us; we watched her as she went up in the elevator, and noticed the special consideration paid by attendants. At home we reckon everybody to be equal, with a few exceptions, but here it was evident that to be called Lady Mirrible counted for something, and we naturally fell in with the local view. When you are in Rome you should do as the Romans do; the remark applies equally well to Florence. The young man gave way to us at the desk of the concierge, and Carolyn Stokes offered him a large smile.

"Have you come far?" she asked.

"Fairly good distance."

"Are you going soon?"

"That doesn't quite depend upon me," he replied.

I mentioned when we were in our room that a considerable amount of information had not been extracted, and Carolyn Stokes said no doubt I should prove more successful in the game. I replied that this seemed highly probable, and we did not speak to each other again until the gong sounded in the corridor announcing that the meal was almost ready. Downstairs in the reading-room we encountered a nasty jar in the discovery that none of the rest of the people had dressed specially for dinner. This was one of the small difficulties caused by the absence of a man capable of making inquiries beforehand.

"I beg your pardon," he remarked. He had taken the Herald from the table just as my hand went out; he replaced it and selected a London journal. I was determined to let Carolyn Stokes see that I could manage the situation better than she had done.

"You are not an American?" I asked.

"I am only English."

"We have met several very pleasant folk from your country in the course of our travels."

"How extremely fortunate."

"What startles us amongst you is your class distinctions. You should, I think, make an endeavour to break down the barriers."

"Something ought certainly to be done," he agreed. And went off with his newspaper.

Carolyn Stokes mentioned not for the first time that she was old enough to be my mother, and went on to argue that whereas it was quite permissible for a woman of her age to speak at an hotel to a stranger, the case was entirely different where a girl of twenty was concerned. All the same when she found him seated at the next table in the dining-room she allowed me to take the chair which enabled me to speak across to him without twisting my neck. From what I heard him say to the waiter I gained that her ladyship was taking the meal in her own room.

Carolyn Stokes has many estimable qualities, but I have more than once had to point out to her that she does not exercise a sufficient amount of restraint over her conversational powers. Also she pitches her voice somewhat high, rather as though she, being at Liverpool, were addressing a public meeting in New York. I am myself a good and fluent talker, but my chances are small if I enter into competition with Carolyn. It was difficult, however, to overlook the fact that he preferred listening to me, and when we both spoke at once it was I who secured his attention. I asked him what there was to be seen in Florence of an evening when the picture galleries were closed, and he said we could not do better than stroll down the Lung 'Arno, see the Vecchio bridge, returning by way of the Piazza Vittore Emmanuele.

"We should scarcely dare to go out alone," I remarked.

He crumbled his bread for a moment.

"I think," he said, "it will be possible for me to place myself at your disposal."

"That is perfectly sweet of you," cried Carolyn Stokes. We arranged to meet at nine o'clock in the entrance hall.

Taking our coffee in the drawing-room Carolyn and myself came to the conclusion that there was more in the wisdom of Providence than some people care to admit. If Mr. Chasemore had decided to come on with us to Florence the likelihood was that we should have had no opportunity of making this very fortunate and delightful acquaintance; there would have been less to record in our diaries under the heading of that day. Carolyn's impression was that the son of a titled lady was a viscount, but she could not be certain; she had on some far-distant occasion studied the matter thoroughly, but most of the information then acquired seemed to have been erased from her mind. Anyway the chance was too good to lose, and Carolyn Stokes said the great thing was to exhibit not too much eagerness, but to allow friendship to ripen, so to speak, in the course of the next twenty-four hours. Carolyn has a distinct streak of sentimentality in her character, and she spoke of the influence of blue Italian skies and the moon shining on the water, and Dante and Beatrice, and the new hat I had purchased in the Via Condotti at Rome. We went upstairs to put on some wraps.

In the passage her ladyship's head was out of her door, and she was calling in an imperative kind of way.

"Norman, Norman! Where on earth has he got to again? Never here somehow when he's wanted." One of the hotel maids came along and she gave her a message. "The lad really," she said, taking her head in, "is perfectly useless."

Carolyn Stokes was occupying a few minutes later a central position at the mirror in our room when she suddenly gave a shriek; I assumed it was only the presence of a moth in the room. As she did not shriek again I considered the hideous danger was past and done with, and I requested her to permit me to share the mirror for a moment.

"Child," she announced in a subdued sort of voice and still gazing into the glass, "I have seen it all in a flash. You are under the impression that he is some sort of a nobleman. He is nothing of the kind. He is merely a footman or a courier, paid a moderate amount per week to attend on this Lady Somebody. That's what he is," she said, striking the dressing table, "and I am more thankful than I can express that I have discovered it in time."

"The question can be easily decided," I mentioned. "We have only to glance in the book kept at the desk below."

"I did that, but they have not yet registered."

"Then a question must be put to the people of the hotel."

"That I also did," replied Carolyn Stokes, "and their acquaintance with the American language made them assume that I required a postcard with a view of the cathedral. They have no right," she went on vehemently, "in these foreign hotels to allow a footman to dine with the other guests. I know it is done, but no one will persuade me that it is right or fair to respectable visitors. It ought to be stopped."

I sat on the rocking chair and took some violent exercise for a few minutes in order to collect my thoughts. It seemed we were in a somewhat difficult corner. To stay in our room only meant that he would come and knock at the door; the wisest plan appeared to be to effect an escape. Carolyn Stokes, for once, agreed with me.

"I wish Mr. Chasemore were here," she said.

We went along the corridor very quietly and crept down the staircase. From the last landing we could see him waiting near the desk of the concierge. There was no means of slipping past without being seen.

"I tell you what to do!" I whispered. "You must go and inform him that I have been taken suddenly ill."

"A good idea," she said, "but I would so much rather you went and told him that I was ill."

He tapped with his walking-stick impatiently on the floor, moved to examine letters in the rack. I pulled at Carolyn Stokes's arm in order to persuade her to make a run for it; before I could arouse her dormant intelligence he had returned to his former position. He glanced at the clock and at his watch; Carolyn Stokes sat on the stairs.

"Meanwhile," I grumbled, "we are missing valuable moments in a most interesting and historical city."

"Think," she said impressively, "think of the fate from which I have saved you."

The call of "Norman!" came again, but apparently it did not reach his ears. I am a creature of impulse and, without thinking, I imitated the call. He whipped off his cap at once, laid down his walking-stick and started up, taking two steps at a time and coming near to us.

Carolyn Stokes and myself will never be able to decide which of us took the initiative, which gripped at the other and used some amount of force. We discovered ourselves in the nearest room, where an elderly gentleman was about to retire to rest; I had never thought the time would come when I should be thankful for not understanding a foreign language.

The young man rushed by; we made our escape just as the aged person was about to throw a hair brush.

We tried to persuade ourselves, in walking along the side of the river, that all was well that ended well. Carolyn Stokes said the experience was one she wished never to undergo again, and for some reason reproached me. We walked as far as the Trinity Bridge, turned to the. left, found ourselves in the Via del Moro, came later to the Piazza de St. Maria Novello, took what we thought would be a short cut for the hotel, and lost ourselves. Carolyn Stokes asked the way of two or three people in tones quite loud enough to enable them to understand, but success did not crown her efforts.

"Why, here you are!" cried an English voice. We turned, and for the moment we both forgot how anxious we had been not to meet him. "Now, how in the world did I manage to miss you? My fault, I'm sure."

"It would be kind of you," said Carolyn Stokes with reserve, "to put us in the right direction for our hotel."

"But, of course, I'll see you back there with the greatest pleasure. Unless you like to allow me, even now, to show you round the town. As a matter of fact, the hotel is just round the corner. There's the Garibaldi statue."

"I am somewhat fatigued," she said, "and I would prefer to return."

"And you?" he said, turning to me.

"There has been a mistake made," I answered resolutely. "We took you for somebody else. You must allow us to close the acquaintance here and now."

"No idea I had a double," he remarked. "This matter must be looked into or complications may ensue."

"We jumped to the conclusion that you were the son of the lady you are travelling with."

"I am," he answered. Carolyn Stokes and I began to talk together; he appeared to do his best to understand us, but presently gave up the attempt and led the way to the hotel. There in the entrance hall he spoke again.

"So it was because I showed some attention to my dear mother that you thought I was a courier."

We interrupted, and endeavoured once more to explain.

"I'm sorry," he said. "Had an idea this was going to be quite a pleasant friendship. Goodbye."

I kept awake half that night making my plans. But in the morning fresh English visitors more titles had arrived, and some of them knew him, and they surrounded him, and the girls made a fuss of him, and there was no chance of my getting near. A letter came for me from Venice saying that the writer would be in Milan on Wednesday. "Yours with affectionate regards, P. A. C."

I have now to rely upon my tact and my industry and my own bright, intelligent young mind to assist me in marrying Mr. Peter A. Chasemore.

X

BEFORE LUNCH

Other travellers were becoming jammed in the corridor of the train, their tempers taking the tone of acerbity easy to those about to start on a railway journey. A determined young woman came up the step, and supported the conductor in an appeal for order, addressing herself more particularly to the English passengers; quiet obtained, she took the first advantage of it by presenting her ticket. The conductor showed gratitude by escorting her at once to her place.

"You don't mean to say—," stammered the occupant of seat Number Twenty. "It can't be! I shall begin to think I'm losing my senses."

"If you're Mr. Chiswell," she replied briskly, "there's no reason to be afraid of that."

"A remark," protested Mr. Chiswell, "so unkind that I can tell it comes from nobody but Miss Everitt." She lifted her bag to the rack, and when she had succeeded in placing it there, he made a gesture of assistance. Glancing at herself in the mirror below the rack, she remarked that she looked a perfect bird frightener.

"I don't agree with you," he said.

"So far as I remember," she said, "you seldom did."

"We won't exaggerate," urged Mr. Chiswell. "For my part, I'm very glad that we're to be fellow travellers, and I trust we shall have a pleasant journey. It's clear enough to me, Miss Everitt, that fate has brought us together again."

"Then I wish to goodness fate would mind its own business."

The last passenger came into the saloon; the conductor's forehead cleared of wrinkles, and he hung up his brown peaked cap with a sigh of relief. The train moved out from the Gare de Lyon in a casual way, as though it were going for a short stroll, and giving no indication that it intended to occupy the day by racing down the map of France. Folk on the low platform of the station waved handkerchiefs, blew kisses, cried.

"Is Freddy with you?" asked Miss Everitt.

"Need you ask! Is Emily with you?"

"Course she is."

"Neither of 'em married?"

"Neither of them married," agreed Miss Everitt. "Just as well perhaps. There are people who, so long as they remain single, can keep up a certain style and position; once they get spliced, first thing they do is to cut down expenses."

"Exactly the view I took of it," he cried eagerly. He leaned forward, and gave a glance around the saloon to make certain that no one listened. "Just the way I looked at the matter. Between ourselves, it was because of that I acted as I did."

The attendant from the dining-car came to inquire whether the passengers wished to lunch in the first series, or in the second series; the two, after consultation, settled to take the meal together at the later hour. They found new grounds for agreement in the view that coffee and rolls at half-past seven in the morning, at a Paris hotel, formed but a mere imitation of a breakfast.

"I know perfectly well that what I'm going to tell you," said Chiswell confidentially, "won't go any further. I recollect how in the old days when we were well, friends you always knew when to keep your mouth shut. A great quality, that, in a girl, and I don't want to flatter you when I say that one very seldom comes across it. What I'm about to tell you refers to—"

He jerked his head, and she nodded.

"They might meet," she said.

"It wouldn't matter," he replied confidently. "They're not on speaking terms now."

"Fire away with what you were going to tell me."

"As a Member of Parliament," began Mr. Chiswell, "Freddy was not what the world might call a roaring success. Used to take a lot of trouble, and the Duke, his old father, was always getting at him, and asking when he was going to be asked to join the Cabinet. As a matter of fact, his speeches sounded all right when he said 'em off to me in Curzon Street, but apparently when he tried 'em in the House they didn't go for nuts. I never went down there to hear him got too much respect for myself to go near the place but I always read the Parliamentary reports, and there, when he did get the chance of speaking, the papers mentioned his name amongst the 'Also spokes' and that was about all. Whatever faults he may have had as a Member of Parliament, he was, and he is, a first-class chap to valet, and I don't care." Mr. Chiswell gave a resolute gesture "I don't care where the next comes from. I've only to say one word against a suit of clothes, and that suit of clothes is virtually handed over to me on the spot. I know to a penny what his income is, and I know to a penny what his expenses amount to. A peculiar chap, mind you, in some ways; never able, for instance, to bear the idea of being in debt. Most extraordinary, with people of his class."

Chiswell dismissed this problem.

"Now you must understand you know me well enough to realise it that I'm not one of those who want to be always chopping and changing. If I'm in a nice comfortable easy chair like this, I'm not the kind of chap to give it up, and go and sit out there in the corridor on a tip-up wooden seat. I'm the sort that—"

"Leave off bragging as soon as you're tired," suggested Miss Everitt, "and get on with your story."

The young man, an elbow resting on the ledge of the window, and giving no attention to the scenery which flew past, with a straight road curling up like a length of white ribbon, applied himself to the task of describing the course of procedure adopted. The girl gave now and again a cough of criticism, here and there a slightly astonished lift of the eyebrows. Occasionally she sniffed at a bottle of Eau de Cologne with the air—obviously copied from some superior model—the air of having temporarily lost interest in the subject. Stated with a brevity that Chiswell, the day before him and personal exultation behind, could not be induced to show, the particulars might be fairly stated thus. Chiswell—

"Mind you," he said firmly, "no one can call me a Paul Pryer. I look after myself; I don't profess to look after others."

—Chiswell happened, by chance, to come across a note addressed to his master which, so far as he could judge, had no reference to his master's Parliamentary duties, or to any scheme for improvement of the masses; he founded his opinion on the fact that it commenced "My dearest." Chiswell, a man of the world, would have been prepared to exercise tolerance and to pass it by with a wink, but for the fact that the communication was dated from an exclusive ladies' club; the fact that the writer adopted a pen name baffled him and aroused his curiosity. He left the letter on the table, and concealed inquisitiveness until he should be entrusted with letters for the post. Looking through the bundle handed to him at four o'clock he felt pained and grieved to find that his master had not trusted him fully and entirely; the envelopes were addressed either to Esquires or to ladies known to the world as seriously interested in the work of the party. He particularly asked whether there were any other communications to be placed in the pillar box for despatch, and his master, on the point of running off to the House, distinctly and formally answered:

"No, Chiswell. That's the lot. Don't forget to post them."

"Quite sure, sir?"

The reply to this polite and deferential question came in the form of a request, first that Chiswell should not be a fool, second that if he could not help being a fool, he would at any rate take steps to hide and to mask the circumstance. Chiswell was affected by these remarks as a duck is concerned by water running over its back; what did perturb him was the want of confidence shown between master and man after an acquaintance that had lasted for years. Chiswell, pondering on this, was placing the letters singly in the pillar box and giving to each a final examination when he discovered that one, addressed

"I know!" said Miss Everitt, much interested.

Bore a special sign on the flap of the envelope. Mr. Chiswell, scarce hoping that he had struck the trail, retained this and kept it back for further consideration.

The custom of placing scarlet wax on the flap of an envelope and impressing the wax with a seal is probably an old-fashioned tradition dating from the days when gum could not be trusted. In the case of an envelope fastened in the ordinary way, Chiswell would have had to take the trouble of placing a kettle on the gas stove; in the present instance his work was rendered easy by the help of a penknife and, later, the use of a stick of wax and the seal. The matter appeared to be serious. A passing flirtation Chiswell might have permitted, although that he would have held undignified in a Member of the House of Commons, but within the few lines of the letter before him there seemed a plain hint of marriage. He was about to tear up the letter in the hope of thus giving a start to a misunderstanding when it suddenly occurred to him

"An inspiration," said Chiswell contentedly. "That's what you may call it."

It suddenly occurred to him that the insertion of two words in the brief note, just two words in a space that seemed to have been left temptingly for them, would entirely alter the meaning: changing it from a hurried message of affection into a hasty intimation of dislike. "Do not" were the two words, and Chiswell took the pen and wrote them as quickly as he now, in the Cote d'Azur express, spoke them.

"You're not blaming me," urged Mr. Chiswell apprehensively.

"Go on," she ordered.

Little else to go on about. The letter, resealed, went to its destination; the General Election came, and that meant a quick departure for the country. Freddy, greatly worried with one matter and another, seemed, so far as his valet could judge, to enter upon the contest in anything but a whole-hearted fashion; Chiswell managed to intercept and cancel a telegram sent to the same young party, urgently begging her to come and help. The meetings were noisy, and the candidate, who but a few years before made retorts which became classical, and delivered speeches the reports of which had to be decorated by reporters with "Loud laughter" and "Long and continued cheering" gave no signs of alertness, falling back on dreary statistics which he himself could not understand, and his audiences declined to accept. Now that it was all over, they were on their way to Nice, where Chiswell hoped to meet no one but other defeated candidates and attendants who, it might be hoped, would, in their own interests, abstain from the vulgar chaff to which he and his master had been subjected in town.

"But what I want to point out to you, my dear beg pardon what I want to say is that I managed to stop him from entering upon marriage, and in doing so, I reckon I did a good turn for myself, and that I did a good turn for you."

"She was very much worried and upset."

Chiswell stretched himself luxuriously.

"It don't do to share other people's anxieties," he said. "Great thing in this world is to keep trouble off your own shoulders. Do that, and you may reckon you've done pretty well. How have you been getting along since since—"

"Since you dropped me?"

"Mutual consent," he argued, rather uneasily, "mutual consent." Both looked out of the window for a time. "By the by, do you ever see anything of that chap Miller? You don't remember him perhaps; he was in Grosvenor Gardens when last I heard of him."

"I believe he's there still," she answered, examining the tips of her boots.

"When did you?"

"Oh, don't bother me!" cried Miss Everitt sharply. "You're always wanting to know everything about everybody. A nuisance, that's what you are."

"I've got no grievance against Miller," contended Chiswell. "You're doing me an injustice. Me and Miller are good friends enough. Last time I met him he gave me some information, and we parted on what I may call the most amicable terms. I shouldn't at all mind," he went on generously, "I shouldn't object in the least to running across poor Miller again."

"You needn't call him 'poor'."

"I'm not using the term," said Mr. Chiswell, "in a monetary sense."

"The monetary sense, as you call it, is about the only one you possess."

Noting that she tapped the side of her easy chair and that her head trembled, he decided to say nothing more on the subject, reverting instead to the matter already discussed. In going over some of the circumstances he found excuse for increased content; the swiftness of his action, and the general dexterity he had displayed made his eyes grow round and bulgy. The dining-car attendant came through to announce that the first series for lunch was ready, and Chiswell said he would smoke one cigarette and then go along and see whether his services were required by Freddy. Miss Everitt rose, remarking that it would be well, perhaps, for her to ascertain, at once, whether she could be of any use to Emily.

They returned to their chairs in less than five minutes: one perturbed, the other calm.

"Well, of all the—" he spluttered.

"What I mean to say is, what in the world is going to happen next, I wonder?"

"That's more than either of us can tell," remarked Miss Everitt composedly. "What I know is that I do want my lunch. Sight of food in the dining-car has made me feel hungry."

"The two of them! The two of them sitting there at a small table opposite each other!"

"I caught sight through the glass door of the bill of fare," said Miss Everitt. "The name of the fish I couldn't quite make out, but there were cotes de bceuf rotis, and poularde, and haricots verts."

"They were sharing a bottle of Chablis together. And he he'd placed his hand on the top of her hand. Did you notice?"

"Wonder whether they'll give us an ice?"

Chiswell found a handkerchief and rubbed his forehead.

"All very well for you to sit there and talk about food; how do you know that now they've met and made it up, that she won't get rid of you in the same way that he's jolly well certain to manage without me?"

"It doesn't matter," she replied, with calm. "I've saved!"

"The amount you've saved, my girl," he declared, "will last you for just about five weeks."

"What do you know about how much I've put by?" she demanded.

"I can tell you the sum to within a pound. I can write it down now, if you'll lend me a lead pencil."

He scribbled some figures on the margin of his newspaper, and handed it across to her.

"Guess again!" she said.

"It isn't a question of guessing," he said. "I happen to know. Unless you've made a considerable sum within the last three months, that's the exact amount."

"You really believed, then, what Mr. Miller told you?"

The conductor came, and returned to each the green cardboard covers enclosing' their tickets. Under the impression that Chiswell was still a blade, a chum, a jovial companion, the conductor aimed at him a cheerful blow on the shoulder, and the train giving at this moment a lurch, the action took something of a more aggressive nature. Chiswell blazed up, trying to disengage himself from his coat. Other passengers in the saloon looked around interestedly; Miss Everitt interposed and ordered Chiswell to behave himself, to remember that he was in the presence of ladies. The conductor apologised and went on; the French passengers remarked to each other that the English formed an excitable nation.

"Pardon me," said Chiswell to his companion, "but I should like to know your facts. I should be very glad indeed if you'll kindly place me in possession of the true circumstances. To put it plainly here's your pencil how much have you actually got in the bank on deposit, or on current account at the present moment? That's all I want to know."

She struck out his figures and wrote underneath. Leaning over he gave a whistle of astonishment.

"My dear," he said deferentially. "There's been a misunderstanding, due to the interference of outsiders. It's not too late to put it all smooth and right again, but at the same time I'm bound to say such conduct is altogether inexcusable. When I come across Miller, I shall tell him so to his face. Who asked him to come to me, and give me wrong information, I should like to know? "

"I did!" she remarked. "But I've just made up for it by giving correct information on another subject to my young mistress."

Chiswell threw himself back in his chair, and gazed severely at the roof of the saloon carriage.

"All I can say is," he declared, "it's absolutely ruined my lunch."

XI

COUNTER ATTRACTIONS

Half the time I don't trouble to look up at them, especially when I happen to be busy. They put their money underneath the brass wire; they ask for what they want; it's given to them, and off they go. If any other plan was adopted we should never get through the work at our office, and there would be complaints to answer, and the superintendent might send some one along to kick up a row. As Miss Maitland says, when all the customers are made on one pattern everything will be much easier to manage; meanwhile we can't do better than to do the best we can, and to recognise that some are in a hurry, some are just the reverse.

"Above all," mentioned Miss Maitland, when I first came here, "no carrying on across the counter with young gentlemen."

"When you've known me longer, Miss Maitland," I said, "you'll see how unnecessary it is to make a remark like that."

"I'm only warning you for your own good."

"I can behave myself," I said, "as well as most girls. The fact that I'm a bit above the average in regard to looks—"

"Is that really a fact?" inquired Miss Maitland.

The very queer thing about it all was that he came in on the afternoon of the very second day I was there. I was having an argument about a halfpenny with a lady sending a telegram, and she said that she always understood we were well paid, and if that was true we ought not to try to make anything extra. I kept my temper, but I daresay I managed to say what I wanted to say I generally do and eventually she took the telegram back and decided to take a cab to Charing Cross and send it from there.

"Shilling's worth of your best stamps," he requested; "I want them to match my necktie."

"Pennies or halfpennies?" I asked. You can understand I wasn't in the mood for nonsense just then."

"Which are most fashionable just now, miss? I don't want to look odd or conspicuous."

"You'll do that in any case. Kindly say what you want."

"Perhaps I'll try sixpenny worth of each," he said.

I tore them off and pushed them underneath the trellis.

"Are these absolutely fresh? I may not be cooking them at once, you see. They'll be all right, I suppose, if I keep them on ice?"

"You may as well put your head there at the same time," I said.

The other girls on my side of the counter looked around, and Miss Maitland gave a cough.

"Heavens!" he said, putting on a deep voice, "how I adore the fair creature! Ere yonder sun sinks to its rest she must, she shall, be mine."

I glanced up at him, prepared to give him such a haughty look, but I found he was a good-tempered-looking young fellow with his straw hat tipped to the back of his head, and somehow I couldn't manage my cold stare quite so well as usual. Two or three people entered through the swing doors at that moment and came straight to my part of the counter.

"Very well then," he said loudly, "that's arranged. Outside the British Museum Tube Station half-past eight to-night. Mind, I shan't wait more than ten minutes."

The fuss Miss Maitland made just because I'd answered him back! I had a good mind to say something about old maids, but I stopped it just in time; instead I thought it the best plan to say he was a great friend of my brother's and that he was one of those peculiar young gentlemen who had the impression that he ought to keep up his reputation for being comic.

"If he comes in again," said Miss Maitland, "call me, and I'll show you how to deal with him."

The next day at about the same time I noticed out of the corner of my eye his lordship at the doors. He came in and I knew he was looking for me; to please Miss Maitland I went along to deal with some registered letters; she left her stool and took my place. "Now," I said to myself, "now he'll get his head bitten off." I was engaged with work for about five minutes, and to my surprise, when I had finished, there was Miss Maitland chatting away with him as amiably as possible. "I like to go somewhere fresh every year," she was saying. "If That's why I went to Windermere last summer." He said, "Not in July by any chance?" and she said, "Yes, the middle of July." It appeared he had been there at that date; not exactly Windermere but at Bowness, and he remarked talking to her in a very different way from the one he had adopted with me that it would have greatly improved his holiday if he had been so fortunate as to meet her. Maity gave a sort of smile and was about to make some further remark when he took out his watch, lifted his straw hat, hurried away.

"Really," she said to me, still flushed with the conversation and looking quite young, "really a very well-spoken gentleman. Depends a good deal on how we approach them. If they think we want silly talk, why naturally enough they give it. In a general way," concluded Maity, as though she possessed a wide and considerable experience, "in a general way men treat us as we deserve to be treated."

He came in again that afternoon to use the telephone; the box was occupied and he had to wait. We were all watching to see how he would behave this time; lo and behold if he didn't take a big book from underneath his arm called The Horse and Us Health and read carefully, taking no notice of any of us. Maity looked disappointed, and one of the girls said the great drawback about men was that they were never twice alike.

That was the evening I found him waiting outside. It always rains when I leave my umbrella at home, and I couldn't very well refuse his offer to see me into the motor omnibus, and it was certainly kind of him to suggest that I should take his gamp. I told him that the bus took me within a minute and a half of mother's house.

At the time I was in the habit of telling mother everything, and she decided not often she praised me that I had behaved in a ladylike manner, and mentioned it would be a good thing if every mother brought up children as she had treated me. Mother told me about one or two half-engagements that occurred before she married poor father, and gave me one piece of advice which she said was worth its weight in gold, namely, that the moment you saw a young man getting fond of you the best plan was to pretend to be indifferent and in this way to make him see that there was a lot of hard work in front of him. Mother said this three times to impress it on my memory.

How in the world he found out the name it was not easy to see, but, as every one is aware, people spare themselves no trouble when they become fond of anybody. However that may be, the fact remains that a letter came, signed W. J. C., saying the writer would be at the statue on a certain day and at a certain hour, and, just for fun, I kept the appointment. Maity was very nice about giving me leave, and I waited there ten minutes. For a full ten minutes nothing happened, and I had to look at the omnibuses as they stopped in order to pretend I wanted to catch one of them. Presently I caught sight of him looking in a newspaper shop, and taking his time over it too. I became so mad that if there had been a pebble about I think I should have picked it up and thrown it at him. He turned, and I had to wave my muff in order to gain his attention.

"Hullo," he said, coming across. "Taking up express messenger-boy work? Where's your parcel?"

"I came here," I said coldly, "because I was asked to do so, and for no other reason. I've no desire to be made to look like an idiot." "Plenty of easier tasks than that," he mentioned. "I should reckon you were one of the most sensible girls going."

"People say that about a lady when they can't think of any other compliment to pay her."

"Are you waiting for anybody, I wonder?" "I wish you wouldn't try to make jokes." "My dear girl," he cried, and he seemed greatly concerned, "please forgive me. And now that we're here, what shall we do?" He looked around, glanced at his watch, and sighed. "Come along and see a bioscope show."

We caught a bus and went to one of the swell places in Oxford Street; I couldn't help feeling pleased when I noticed that he paid eighteenpence each for seats. You can say what you like, and you can talk about the joys of being independent, but there's something very gratifying in discovering for the first time that a gentleman is willing to take your ticket for you. Of course the place was all darkened whilst the pictures were going on, and I thought perhaps he would try to take my hand, and I was prepared to give him a pretty sharp remark if he did; but nothing happened, and I couldn't make it out at all. It was nothing like what I'd read in books; nothing like what other girls had told me.

"You seem a very comfortable set in your office," he said when the lights went up. "All on good terms with each other, aren't you?"

"I suppose so," I answered. "It's my first experience, you see. What age do you think I am?"

"I should say that you are young enough to be pleased if I guessed you to be older than you really are. Shall we say nineteen?"

"Eighteen next birthday, and that's on Tuesday of next week." (There's nothing like giving a hint.)

"What have you been doing all these eighteen years?"

"Improving myself," I said.

"You can give that up now you are perfect."

The lights went down again, and there was a set of pictures about a girl who was being loved by two gentlemen one rather plain with plenty of money and the other much better-looking but apparently only a clerk. I thought over his last remark and tried to discover whether he was still joking or whether he really meant it if he did mean it it was a very gratifying thing to be said, especially in view of the fact that mother is generally finding fault with me. She has often said that I'm the worst girl in the world for leaving my shoes about and not putting a book away when I have done with it, and all this going on day after day, week after week, had given me a kind of a lurking suspicion that I wasn't quite up to the mark. When the pictures showed that the plain man's money really belonged to the good-looking chap he began to talk again and went back once more to the subject of the post office. I would rather he had spoken of something else; I wanted to forget Maity and the rest of them for awhile.

"Are many of them engaged?" he asked.

"Two of them say they are," I replied. "I should feel inclined to guess it was only a half-and-half affair in either case."

"Wonder what their names are?" I told him and he seemed relieved. "It's very strange," he went on, speaking in a more serious way than usual, "how these affairs happen. Looks as though some one who exercises control jumbles all the names into two hats and picks out one from each at random and decides that they shall meet each other and fall in love."

"A good deal of it is mere luck," I agreed. "Mother met father at a dance at the Athenaeum up at the end of Camden Road. Of course a steward introduced them, but to all intents and purposes they were strangers."

"A man goes on," he said, still thoughtfully, "fighting pretty hard and not giving much attention to the other sex and all at once he catches sight of a face, through, say, brass trelliswork, and instantly he decides 'That's the girl for me'. And he thinks of nothing else, can't keep away from the neighbourhood of her, and—" He put his hands over his eyes and bent down.

I felt sorry and I felt pleased if you understand that; sorry for him, pleased for myself seemed as though I had done him an injustice. It showed that you could not reckon any one up correctly by their outside manner. At the first I had no idea he was anything but the ordinary chaffing sort of young gentleman, and here he was obviously upset. All very well for mother to say that you ought to keep them at arm's length when they are fond of you, but I simply couldn't help patting his sleeve gently.

"Thanks very much," he said gratefully. ' You're a good little girl and I'm really obliged to you."

There was a funny set after this, with a short-sighted old gentleman blundering over everything he did, getting mixed up with motor cars, carried up by a balloon, tumbling down the funnel of a ship, and finally being rolled out flat by a steam roller, and pulling himself together and walking off.

"Always feel sorry for people who have to wear glasses," I remarked.

"It improves some people."

"I don't agree with you. See how peculiar our old joker looks at the office."

He stared at me.

"Surely you don't mean that, Miss Maitland?" he said.

"Of course I mean that Miss Maitland. Who else should I be referring to?"

He pressed the palm of a hand against his forehead.

"Let us get this straight," he urged. "We seem to be in a muddle. Your name is Haltland, isn't it?"

"My name is Barnes. Up to the present."

"Then that confounded new messenger boy took my shilling and mixed up the information, and—" he stopped and fanned himself "and you received the letter I intended for her."

"I wish to goodness," I said forcibly, "that some of you men had got a little more common sense."

Mother says everything in this world happens for the best, and in all probability there's some one else waiting for me somewhere. Mother says I have plenty of time in front of me; mother herself was twenty-eight before she married. Mother says there is no need for me to feel nervous until I get past that age.

XII

HERO OF HAMMERTON STREET

He had been away so long that few people remembered him, but his last exploit before leaving ensured that in the minds of those few he remained clear and definite. His wife, when she set out to meet him, was accompanied by a Reception Committee of three, and as they waited outside the large building where he had been staying for the last few months (his hosts kept several important establishments in various parts of the country and he had spent part of the time at one, part at others), as they waited, I say, under the avenue of trees well away from the front door having, as a point of delicacy, no desire to be seen by the servants about the place they speculated on the probable improvement in his personal appearance. Members of the Committee recalled precedents where So-and-so went away stout and unhealthy on a vacation of similar length, and came back so trim and brown that his own sweetheart would not have known him had she remained in the neighbourhood.

"Here he is!" cried the wife suddenly. "I could tell him, bless 'is heart, in a thousand"

"That ain't him!"

"He's got a short beard, at any rate," urged the wife, admitting her error grudgingly as the visitor was claimed and marched off by another lady.

"They all 'ave. Try to use your intelligence, why don't you!"

"Well," said the wife, pointing her umbrella at a sharp-eyed man, who, coming out of the large doorway, glanced around suspiciously, "well, at least that's not my Jim." The sharp-eyed man came across the open space towards them, still keeping a look-out on either side. "He's mistaking us for his own people. My Jim's a better-looking man than him."

"If you say that again, Meria," remarked the arriving man in tones that could not be mistaken, "I shall have to Now then, now then! I don't want no kissing!"

He was dressed in a suit for which he had not been measured, and his boots were scarcely a precise fit; he shambled along with his friends, responding gruffly to their polite inquiries and complaining bitterly first, that they should have come to meet him; second, that so many friends were absent. Informed that some of these were no longer alive, he declined to accept this as a sufficient excuse, describing them as a cantankerous lot, ever thoughtless where the feelings of others were concerned. They stopped quite naturally at the first place of refreshment, and he criticised the beverage set before him, declaring that had he known beer could be so bad, he would not have worried his thoughts so much about it during recent years. He was equally dissatisfied with his first pipe of tobacco, which he had some trouble to light, and when he heard that his sister had married a respectable fruiterer, off Bethnal Green Road, he made no attempt to conceal his annoyance with the way the world had been managed during his absence.

"Once I turn my back for a moment," he said disgustedly. "Who's got the pub at the corner of our street?"

"I've moved, James," explained his wife apologetically.

"Moved? Who told you to move?"

"The landlord, dear."

"Don't you begin 'dearing' of me," he retorted threateningly. "Why wasn't I asked?"

"There was no opportunity, James".

"Bah!" he said, in the manner of one who can find no other repartee. He turned to the men. "What 'ave you three come all the way down ere' for? On the make, I s'pose?"

"We are not on the make," said the leader precisely. "Recollecting what you was put away for, we have come down 'ere to offer you, as something in the nature of a hero, a 'earty welcome on your return to what we may venture to term your 'earth and 'ome." James relaxed the sternness of his demeanour, and took another sip from his glass, this time without making a wry face. "We're a-going to make a fuss of you, old man."

"Don't go overdoing it," he said grudgingly.

They reached Hoxton at about noon, not because the way was long, but because the Committee, possessing funds, desired to do the thing well. A neighbour had taken charge of the arrangements for dinner, and the three men, arrived at the door in Hammerton Street, mentioned gracefully that the reunited pair would in all probability like to be left alone for a few hours, and withdrew; first, however, warning James that he would be expected at the Green Man that evening at eight o'clock precisely, at which hour a few select friends would be present to wish him success in his future career.

"Whad ye mean by my future career?" he demanded. "What are you three a-getting at now?"

"If It's all right, old chap," they answered soothingly. "Only a form of speech, you know."

"Be a bit more careful how you pick your words," he retorted threateningly. "I 'aven't come back to be ragged by such as you."

He was still rather surly that evening when he made his appearance at the Green Man; he explained to one who was formerly his closest friend that he had been enjoying a bit of a talk with the wife. Surroundings in the clubroom were, however, so congenial that before long he showed guarded signs of amiability, albeit he found grounds for annoyance in the fact that some of his old companions had prospered, and had given up what was referred to as the old game to engage on sport that, relatively speaking, was of an honest, law-abiding character. His best friend indeed owned a large gold chain and a watch at the end of it; he was now a bookmaker by profession, not, of course, a literary person, but one who made money. On James suggesting they might perhaps go into partnership together in the racecourse business, the closest friend said, with some reserve, that it was an occupation requiring years of patient study, and -the fact of James having been out of the movement so long barred him both from participating in the profits or sharing the losses.

"See what I mean, don't you?" asked the bookmaker. "Chuck that what you're smoking away, and have a real cigar!"

"I shan't give you another opportunity," said James curtly. "Should have thought you would have been glad of a pretty sharp man for your right 'and."

"But you've been rusting," pointed out the bookmaker. ("Now you've been and bitten off the wrong end.")

Nothing, however, could exceed the geniality of the hosts. Thick crusty sandwiches rested on the deal tables; there was no stint, so far as the guest of the evening was concerned, in regard to liquids. Everybody crowded around him in a flattering way and everybody shook him by the hand several times; a few promising younger men, who were brought up and introduced, showed themselves highly sensible of the honour, and asked eagerly what adventure he thought of going in for next.

"Aven't quite made up me mind," he replied cautiously.

The younger men winked knowingly at each other, saying that James was a deep one and no mistake, adding that an ability to keep one's head shut was a gift to be envied. They had singing later. Songs were given which for James (who had no musical tastes) should at least have possessed the charm of novelty; the slang contained in them and in the public speech of many of those present was to him quite incomprehensible. They repeated unceasingly that they wished him well, and the bookmaker made a speech just before closing time in which he pointed out that every manjack present was prepared to give James a helping hand. Never should it be said of them that they had refused a helping hand to one of the best. A helping hand was due to such a hero and a helping hand he should have.

"Friends, one and all," said James. (He refused for some minutes to make a speech, but gave in to encouragement.) "Friends, one and all."

A cry of "So you said!" and reproving shouts of "Order!"

"I've been away from you fer a few year owin' to owin' to circs not altogether under my control." (the room laughed uproariously), "but I'm back in the midst of you once more, and I can tell you one thing, and that ain't two, I'm jolly glad of it! I've had quite enough penal to last me my time. I'm full up of it! I've reached me limit! It's no catch, I tell you!' (Murmurs of sympathy.) "If there's any one 'ere that's acquired a taste for it, they're welcome to my share. I don't know that I have much more to say. I 'aven't had much practice at public speaking of late. Once you begin to 'old forth in there." (here he gave a vague jerk of the head), "why, they let you know it. Anyway, it's no use 'arping on the past, and in regard to the promise of a 'elping 'and to which you, Mr. Chairman, have so kindly referred, and to me being a hero, there's only one thing I want to say, and that is this: I shall keep you to it!"

The club-room seemed to think the last sentence had an ungracious sound, and there would have been an inclination to hedge only that the white-sleeved potman arrived at that moment with a dictatorial shout of "Now you cheps! Time!" and the party had to break up. Out in the street, James's arm was again in request, and his hand was shaken so often with so many assurances of admiration and enthusiastic comradeship, that he went off towards Hammerton Street quite dazed and not sure whether he had won a battle, or saved lives from drowning. The men cheered him as he left and began to chant an appropriate song, but a policeman came up, and the crowd, not wishful for argument with the force, said respectfully, "It's all right, Mr. Langley, sir; we're just on the move," and disappeared.

Womenfolk came round to Hammerton Street the next day asking to be permitted to see him, and James's wife would have taken another day off, but James said there had been quite enough gadding about for her already, and insisted she should go to work. He sunned himself at the front door with a fine pretence of not knowing that he was being observed, the while women on the opposite side of the pavement held up their babies to see him and whispered admiring comments.

"You'd never think it to look at him, would you, now?"

"I recollect his case as well as anything. It was before I was married to my present 'usband, but I can recollect it all just as though it was only yesterday. I remember so well saying to my young sister I was on speaking terms with her just then I remember saying, 'Ah, well!' I said. Just like that!"

"She's kept herself to herself, mind you, all the time he's been away. I will say that for her!"

"Wonder what he'll be up to now. He's turning something over in his mind, I lay!"

The hero could not help being pleased with all this attention, and after he had taken his dinner at a coffee-shop, where the waitress, informed of his distinguished reputation, stood back and watched him over an illustrated paper, he put on a collar and again lounged at the doorway. The crowd was not so great now, and consisted for the greater part of children who played tip-cat, and gave no notice to him excepting when his presence interfered with the game. Disappointed with his audience, James went indoors and, taking off his collar, indulged hi the unaccustomed luxury of an afternoon nap. When his wife returned from work it struck him that she was slightly more argumentative in manner than she had been on the first day; in the course of debate she threw out a most disconcerting hint in regard to a job of work, news of which had come to her ears.

"Look 'ere, my gel!" said James definitely. "You may as well understand me fust as last. A man with so many friends as I've got won't want to work for many a long day yet."

Nevertheless the idea gave him perturbation and he went round to the Green Man to meet the friends referred to and receive from them reinforcement of his hopes and views. There were only two or . three in sight, and these were outside the house; they hailed him with a casual cry of, "'Ullo, James! Your turn to stand drinks, ain't it?" and having brought some money out, the savings of his compulsory retreat, he found himself compelled to entertain them.

"And what you think of doing now, James," they asked. ("Here's luck!")

"Well," he said slowly, "I s'pose eventually I shall 'ave to find, as the missis says, something or other. But not yet for a month or two."

"You'll probably discover a chance of—"

"No," said James with emphasis. "Not me! No more jobs on the cross for this child. Risks are too great."

"But you don't mean to say that you're going to chuck it?" The men were so much amazed that their glasses remained in mid-air.

"If you guess again," said James stolidly, "you'll be wrong."

He looked about in Hoxton the rest of the evening for friends, and looked about in vain. The next day he called on his closest friend, the bookmaker; the bookmaker was just off to Kempton Park and in peril of losing a train at Waterloo. He had heard, it seemed, of James's decision, and James could trace no sign of the generous friendship previously expressed. To James's suggestion that he should accompany the bookmaker to Kempton Park, and enjoy a day at the other's expense, the reply came prompt and definite. "That be 'anged for a tale!" said the bookmaker.

On the following Monday James went to ask about the job of work to which his wife had referred; all his worst fears were confirmed when he found himself successful in obtaining it.

"Drawback of being an 'ero is," said James gloomily, "that it don't last much more than about five minutes."

XIII

DAMAGES FOR LIBEL

"A rare rush whilst it lasts," mentioned Mrs. Crowther, assisting in the task of clearing tables. "My dear husband used to reckon up how much we should be making profit in a year if, instead of being from twelve to two, it went on from what he called early morn to dewy eve." She sighed. "Mr. Crowther had a lot of poetry in his disposition much more so than most eating-house keepers in Millwall."

"Did he make bits up out of his own 'ead?" asked the girl deferentially.

"Ethel," said the proprietress, nursing a column of plates and speaking with resolution, "you're new to the place, and you're not full acquainted with the rules. Understand, once for all, please, that I don't allow a word to be said against my late husband nor whispered."

"Here's a stray customer coming in, ma'am," remarked the assistant. "Give me that armful, and you see to him."

A stout man, after examining the day's announcement outside, entered and sat down with the relieved air common to those who have walked a great distance and to those who find in any form of exercise a source of trouble; he took off his hat, hung up his overcoat, and said, with relish, "Here comes the busy part of my day!"

Mrs. Crowther rested one palm on the table and gazed at the reversed notice on the window: "The Best of Everything and Everything of the Best," giving him the space to make up his mind.

"You've got a nice little show here."

"Not bad, sir," she replied briefly. "What can I get for you?"

"Been all done up recently, too, if I mistake not. If it hadn't been that I remembered it was exactly opposite the entrance to the works I shouldn't have recognised it. Spent some of the 'appiest hours of my life, I did, over the way."

"The steak and kidney pudding is off," she said, glancing over his shoulder. She took the bill of fare from his hand and deleted the entry, returning the pencil to its position in the fastening of her blouse. Frowning at the impetuosity exhibited, he gave an order. She left, and returned with the liver and bacon and a basket containing squares of household bread.

"Any idea where my old friend Crowther is at the present moment?" he asked jovially. "Him and me were great chums in the old days that are past and done with."

"He's gone."

"Where to?"

She pointed upward reverently.

"That isn't exactly the place where I should have thought of looking for him."

"What do you mean by that?" she demanded sharply.

"Oh, nothing," he said, beginning to eat. "Only very few of us in this world, ma'am, if you don't mind putting yourself out of the question, can be looked upon as perfect. My name's Hards," he went on, his mouth full. "Hards, with an aitch. Daresay you've heard him mention me. I'm speaking now of what shall I say? four, or it might be the early part of five. We were what they call inseparable, him and me, at that period."

"Crowther gave up all his former companions when I married him. "

"He used to complain that you ruled him with a rod of iron."

"I only wish," she declared vehemently, "that the dear man was here to contradict you."

"Crowther was the sort of chap," said the other, with deliberation, "who'd contradict anything. Never better pleased than when he was arguing that black was white. I've known Crowther say one thing to a girl one minute, and another the—"

The customer found his plate snatched away, the remainder of his chunk of bread swept to the floor.

"Go off out of my dining-rooms," she ordered. "Don't you stay here another minute, or else I may use language that I shall be sorry for afterwards, and that you'll be sorry for afterwards. There's your hat, hanging up just behind you. Now move, sharp!"

The sleeves of his overcoat, owing to some defect in the lining, were difficult to manage, and this gave him time to protest. He had come, he declared, with no other intention than that of giving patronage to an establishment which he remembered, with affection, in the time of Crowther's mother, and to enjoy a talk over the past; if, in the course of conversation, he had over-stepped the mark, no one regretted it more acutely than himself. A plain man, accustomed to speaking his mind, he often found that he gave offence where none was intended.

"Jack Blunt they used to call me over at the works," he added penitently. "Owing to me having the awk'ard trick of always telling the truth!"

Mrs. Crowther so far relented as to call the new girl; she instructed her to attend to the customer the while she herself retired to the back to wash up dishes. Mr. Hards said in a whisper to the attendant: "Don't seem to have quite pulled it off, first go!" and Ethel, also in an undertone, replied: "Mustn't get discouraged, uncle. Mother always says it's your one fault. Unsettle her mind about him, that's what you've got to do."

He read a newspaper after the meal, and sent to the proprietress a deferential inquiry, asking whether he might be allowed to smoke, and presently hit upon a device for securing another interview.

"Your memory seems not quite what it ought to be," said Mrs. Crowther, following him to the doorway. "If I were you I'd see a chemist about it."

"I should have recollected that I hadn't settled up," he declared, "just about as I was coming up from the subway at Greenwich." He found corns. "No," gazing at a shilling reverently, "mustn't let you have that one with the hole through it. I was told it would bring me luck. Crowther was wrong for once, but he meant well."

"Did that really once belong to my dear husband?" she asked, with eagerness. "Oh, do let me look. I'd give almost anything to be allowed to keep it."

"Kindly accept it, ma'am, as a present from me, and as a kind of apology for the blunder I made just now."

"I treasure everything he left behind," said Mrs. Crowther tearfully, "since he went, last December, and I don't know in the least how to thank you. Drop in any day you're passing by, and let's have another quiet chat; I'm never 'appier than when I'm talking about him. "

"My time's practically my own," answered Mr. Hards. "Since I retired from over opposite, owing to a slight disagreement years ago, I've done a bit of work, book-canvassing, but that don't take up the entire day. So long!"

A few of the men came into the restaurant, after leaving the works; these were folk who had no expectations of finding tea or supper waiting at home, and they would have stayed on in comfort, gazing admiringly at the young proprietress, only that Mrs. Crowther offered a broad hint by instructing Ethel to find the shutters. They were drifting off, reluctantly, and one was saying to the rest that he would certainly make a dash for it (implying by this that he would make a proposal of marriage) if the lady were not so obviously devoted to a memory, when Mr. Hards appeared at the doorway, heated and exhausted by the effort to arrive before closing time. With him a shy-looking companion, who had to be taken by the arm because he exhibited inclination to refrain, at the last moment, from entering. "Be a sport," urged Mr. Hards. The other intimated by his manner that the task was, for him, considerable.

"Looking younger than ever," declared Mr. Hards effusively. "How are you, ma'am, by this time? Still keeping well? Allow me to introduce you to my friend Ash ton."

"Very pleased," said Mrs. Crowther with a nod. "What will you gentlemen take tea or coffee?''

"Don't suppose," he remarked still in complimentary tones, "that we shall be able to tell any difference. Ashton, you decide."

Ashton, looking around, inquired whether the place did not possess a licence; Mrs. Crowther gave the answer, and he said that perhaps coffee would do him as little harm as anything.

"Happened to run across him," explained Mr. Hards, "and mentioned that I'd met you by chance, ma'am, and he says 'Not the widow of silly old Millwall Crowther?' he says. Just like that. Didn't you, Ashton?"

Mrs. Crowther turned abruptly, and went to furnish the order. "Mind you say 'yes' to everything," ordered Hards privately and strenuously, "or else I'll make it hot for you."

The two greeted Mrs. Crowther with frank and open countenances.

"The late lamented," went on Mr. Hards, with a confidential air, "as you may or may not be aware, used to be in the 'abit of paying attentions to my friend Ashton's sister."

"I know all about that," she remarked curtly. "It was before he met me."

"And, realising how anxious you was to get hold of everything that once belonged to him, I persuaded him to hop off home and have a search. And lo and behold," producing a small paper parcel from the inside pocket of his overcoat, "he found this." Mr. Hards untied the string with deliberation. "There you are!" triumphantly. "Pearls from the Poets. And inside, his handwriting."

"Not sure that I want anything that he gave away to another lady at a time when him and me were not acquainted."

"The date 'll settle that," said Hards. "Ashton, your eyes are younger than mine; what do you make of it?"

Ashton recited the entry with an emphasis on the date; Mrs. Crowther grabbed at the book, glanced at the writing, and sat down on the nearest chair, gazing steadily at a ginger ale advertisement.

"Don't tell me," begged Hards distressedly, "that I've put my foot into it again. Ton my word, if I ain't the most unlucky chap alive. If I'd had the leastest idea that I was going to be the means of disclosing to you the circumstance that Crowther gave away presents of this kind, and with this sort of remark, after he was married to you, why, I'd sooner—"

She started up with the book, and, selecting the fly-page, placed this between her eyes and the gas-light.

"Some one's been altering the date," she said quietly. She threw the volume across. "You gentlemen have got just two minutes and a half before we close for the night. And, as the business is doing pretty well, perhaps you don't mind if I suggest you never show your faces inside here again." She went.

"Any objection to me offering you a word of advice, old man?" asked Ashton, on the pavement. "You're on the wrong tack. When a woman's made up her mind, the best plan is to agree with her. What you ought to do?"

"Keep quiet," ordered the other exasperatedly. "Can't you see I'm thinking?"

They crossed, and walked beside the blank wall of the works.

Ashton was again invited, in plain language, to preserve silence by putting his head in a bag. The lights went out in the restaurant opposite; on the first floor a match was struck and applied to the gas globes; the music of a pianoforte was heard.

"It's a shame," declared Hards, throwing out his arms emphatically, "a right-down shame for a nice-looking young woman of her sort to be left alone and neglected. Here she is, able to cook, able to play, very good to look at, and she's no business to be left by herself."

"Evidently she don't want to be left with you."

"You hop off home," ordered Hards, "soon as ever you like, and take that book with you, and don't you ever attempt to interfere again with matters you've got no concern in. Otherwise—"

His friend hurried away without taking the opportunity to hear the alternative.

Mr. Hards waited until his niece came out with a letter for the post. A whistle brought her to him from the pillar-box.

"Who was it addressed to?" he demanded. The girl replied that she had omitted to look. "'Ton my word," he cried, "I seem to be surrounded by lunatics. Nobody's got a particle of sense, so far as I can ascertain, excepting myself. No wonder I can't manage matters as I should like. But, putting all that on one side, what I want now is another interview with her."

"Judging by what she said after you left, you're not likely to get it."

"Look here, my girl. It was your own mother's suggestion at the start, and she won't be best pleased if you make yourself a stumbling-block. She, for some reason, seems to have got tired of me living in her house at Greenwich, and it was her idea I should marry well, and settle down somewhere else. Apart from which, I've arrived at a time of life when I need a woman's care and good feeding, and enough money in my pocket to stand treat to friends after they've stood treat to me." He spoke distinctly. "I'm going to knock at that door over there presently, and you've got to let me in, and you can stand by and listen whilst I say a few words, and put it all on a proper footing."

"But she hates the very sight of you."

"The sort of sensation," he declared, "that can soon be turned to love."

Mr. Hards thought it wiser, on finding himself outside the door of the restaurant, to give a sharp double knock. He smiled contentedly on hearing young Mrs. Crowther's voice call out: "It's all right, Ethel. Only the postman. I'll answer him!" She opened the door, and faced him with a look of expectancy that at once vanished.

"Excuse me, ma'am," he said, taking off his hat, "but I've been speaking my mind to that young fellow, and he asked me to call back and apologise on his behalf. I never noticed what he'd been up to, altering that date; it wanted a lady's sharpness and a lady's intelligence to detect that. What he wants me to say is he acted on the impulse of the moment."

"He'd better give up acting altogether," she remarked. "Did you really know my husband well, or was it all gas?"

"Didn't I never tell you about that affair poor Crowther and me had with a bobby down near the London Docks one night in November? A fine chap," went on Hards reminiscently, "if ever there was one. The way he could put up his dooks whenever there was trouble about! I seldom met a fellow who was his equal. He was what I call a manly man. When they told me he'd gone and left you a widow I cried like a child, I did."

"I was upset at the tune," remarked Mrs. Crowther, "but it soon wore off."

"It's often struck me," he went on, surprised, "that perhaps you didn't appreciate him at his true value whilst he was alive. Very likely you don't know, as I know, the way he used to talk about you behind your back."

"If it was anything like the way he talked in front of my face, I'd rather not hear."

"Anyway, I daresay, ma'am, you often find yourself looking about for his successor?"

"To tell you the truth, I do."

He tried to take her hand, but failed.

"I can see him now," he remarked sentimentally. "We was walking together in Stratford Broadway, and suddenly he turned to me and he says, 'Ernest,' he says, 'something seems to tell me I'm not long for this world. I want you to make me a promise,' he says. 'If anything amiss happens to me, I look to you to be a friend to the wife. And if so be,' he says, with a sort of a kind of a break in his voice, 'if so be as you should take a fancy to her, and she should take a fancy to you, nothing would give me more pleasure looking down on you both, he says, 'than to—'"

"Bequeathed me to you, did he?"

"It amounts to that, ma'am."

"All this is news to me,' she remarked. "About what date was it?"

"About what date?" echoed Hards, rubbing his chin. "I can give it you within a very little. It was the night before I met William Humphries, and him and me had a few friendly words about football, and I was in the hospital for three weeks. That was the early part of December. I think it was December you said that poor Crowther drew his last breath. Must have been only a few days three at the utmost that he had his talk with me."

"That seems strange."

"Strange things do occur in this world."

"Because Crowther was laid up in his last illness for four months inside this house, and never went outside until the undertaker's man carried him. And a pretty tidy nuisance he was, too, then, and, in fact, all the time I was married to him. Is that a constable coming along, or a postman?"

Hards, having ascertained that the approaching man did not represent the law, remained, searching his mind busily. The postman stopped, gave Mrs. Crowther a letter with a foreign postmark, and remarked that the evening was fine.

"His ship will be home here within a fortnight," she cried excitedly, glancing at the first words of the communication. 'Twa weeks from to-day."

"Who?"

"Nobody you know," said Mrs. Crowther. "And then we shall be married, and I shan't have to keep the men at the works off by pretending to be so fond of my first. It's taken a bit of doing. Let me think, now. You want to see Ethel, I expect, don't you?"

"I don't want to see no one," he declared with an emphatic gesture, "no one on this side of the river ever again, so long as I jolly well live!"

XIV

THE REST CURE

"Knew you'd like it, dear," said Mr. Gleeson confidently. "I declared the moment I saw the place, 'Now this,' I said to myself, 'this will suit the dear wife down to the ground. Just look at that bit over there. (Wait a moment, driver.) Isn't that simply—"

He gave a gesture which meant that the English language provided no adequate words. His wife, with one hand upon his shoulder, offered an "Ah!" of content.

"'You must paint this," he went on, recovering powers of speech. "You must bring your easel and your white umbrella some morning when I'm busy, and try to get this effect. See the top of the church spire above the trees?"

"That there's a oast house," interrupted the driver.

"You will not forget that I shall have my duties in the village," she reminded him. "We are going to make life brighter, you know, for everybody."

"True!" he admitted. "It will require discretion."

"And diplomacy."

"Still, we're not exactly amateurs. We bring something like a ripe experience to the task. This will be child's play after London. Think of the difference in numbers. Driver, how many inhabitants are there in Murford Green?"

"Can't say as I ever counted 'em."

"But speaking approximately." "Well," said the driver, with deliberation, "speaking approximately, I should say they was no better than they ought to be. And you'll excuse me, but I've got to get back to meet the five-eight, and if you and your lady could give me what you may call permission to go on now without any more pulling up, I shall jest do it. Otherwise I shan't, and then Miss Bulwer won't let me never hear the last of it. That's what she won't!"

"Who is Miss Bulwer?"

"Look 'ere," argued the driver, half turning in his seat. "I've answered a pretty tidy number of questions sence we started from the railway station, and I'm beginning to lose my voice, and I'm not far off from losing my temper. But in reference to your question concerning, or regarding, or affecting Miss Bulwer, my answer is, you'll jolly soon find out! Is that good enough for you, or isn't it?"

"Merely a surface manner," explained Mr. Gleeson, as the open fly trundled on again.

"You don't know these people, my dear. A certain veneer of brusqueness, but underneath that good pure gold. Simple natures, I admit, but as honest and straightforward—Wonder," dropping his voice, "wonder how much he expects for this journey?"

"Pay him well," suggested young Mrs. Gleeson, also in a whisper. "We must make a good impression at the start. Say eighteen-pence."

"Fortunately," resuming ordinary tones, "both you and I will be protected and saved by our keen sense of humour." He smiled. "I expect our arrival will nutter Murford Green pretty considerably. On an even surface the slightest ripple shows."

Both stood up in the open carriage on finding that the prophecy seemed to receive full justification. Twenty or thirty men and lads were rushing across the triangle of green, shouting wildly; in their hands they carried stout hammers and long-handled axes; women cheered from doorways of cottages. A few were distracted temporarily by sight of the station fly, but, reproved by the others, they went on, atoning for the slight delay by shrieking more loudly than the rest.

"Anything on, driver?"

"Something coming off," answered the man. "I said what'd 'appen when people began to lock up gates that'd been open for generations and generations. I warned 'em, but they wouldn't take no notice. And I ain't of 'en wrong, neither," concluded the driver.

"Don't be frightened, dear," urged Mr. Gleeson. "I'll go out presently and set it to rights. One wise word from an impartial person, and it will all be over."

The driver said at the destination that, times without number, he had received three and six for the service, paid willingly; if the gentleman had no more silver he supposed he would have to be content with three shillings.

In reply to contentions, the driver asked whether Mr. Gleeson was aware of the price being asked, at the present moment, for oats, and Mr. Gleeson having to admit that his knowledge on this subject was incomplete, the driver retorted, "Very well then, what's the use of arguing? Why not pay up and look pleasant over it?" The fare obeyed the first part of this recommendation. The two maids (sent on in advance from Kensington) stood inside the gate, and caught the driver's farewell remark.

"Really, ma'am," said the elder primly, "the manners of these people! I thought I knew something about language, but I've learnt something the three days we've been down here. Had a pleasant journey? Me and Sarah have both been feeling humpish. I told her it would be all right soon as ever you and the master came."

Mr. Gleeson set out, immediately after a meal, to arrange the question that was troubling Murford Green. He had changed into a Norfolk suit, and as a further concession smoked a briar pipe; with a thick walking stick he prodded at dock-leaves on the green. Near one corner of the triangle a meeting was being held, with a large-faced man shouting excitedly from a Windsor chair. Mr. Gleeson crossing over, added himself to the audience. "Well spoke," sang the crowd, as the large man appeared to finish. "Very well putt!"

"There's my shop 'cross there," shouted the orator, pointing to windows that had "Crutchley, Butcher," in marble letters overhead. "If any one thinks I've broke the law, that's where they can serve a summons."

The crowd looked around at the village constable. The constable frowned with the air of a man who had not entirely succeeded in making up his mind.

"We've got our rights," the butcher went on, "and I defy any one to say the contrairy. If there's anybody here who don't agree with me, now's the time for him to step up and express his opinion. Free speech is our motto and What name, please?"

"My name is Gleeson," announced the newcomer, "and I should like to say a few words."

"For the agitation, may I ask, or against?"

"My attitude," said Mr. Gleeson, "is that of a peace-maker."

The crowd grumbled; the butcher called for order. Mr. Gleeson ascended the chair.

When, at the end of ten minutes, he stepped down, only the constable was there to give him a hand. The constable accounted for the dispersal of the crowd by pointing out that supper time was near, and on Mr. Gleeson asking whether he thought the words spoken had produced any effect, replied, cautiously, that it was difficult to say. The constable, as one who had looked on at many struggles, gave the opinion that you could not do better than let the parties fight it out and, this done, then possibly, but not certainly, came the moment for you to interfere. Mr. Gleeson felt bound, in reply, to mention that he had in his time been called to the bar; intimated that, in circumstances such as these, it seemed more fitting that he should give advice than take it.

"Now," admitted the constable, "now you're putting a different light, sir, on the matter. To tell the truth, I wasn't quite aweer who I was talking to. I look on your arrival here, sir, as particular fortunate, because you can back me up in any action I see fit to take."

"Any correct action."

"That's the only way I've got of doing things. I've never yet made a blunder, and I don't suppose now I ever shall."

"We are all of us liable to err," pointed out Mr. Gleeson.

"Being liable to do a thing," retorted the constable judicially, "and actually doing it, is two entirely different matters. Shall I tell you, sir, what idea has just come into my head?"

Permission given.

"This is the way I get 'old of notions," went on the other self-exultantly. "I may be walking along a quiet lane, or standing here, as I am now, and all at once they come into my noddle like a well, more like a flash of lightning than anything else. It's won'erful. Gives me quite a turn for the moment. Guess what the notion is that I've just thought of."

The gentleman from London excused himself from making the attempt, and found his arm hooked confidentially by the handle of the policeman's stick.

"I'll bring over to your 'ouse this very evening two of the leaders of this movement, or agitation, or whatever you like to call it. You take down their evidence and to-morrow you go and call on Miss Bulwer. She's the lady who's been trying to stop up this path. You talk it over with her, you do, and settle it, and then announce your decision. As easy," concluded the policeman, detecting hesitation, "as easy as saying the A.B.C."

Two days later the constable, on receiving news from Crutchley, Butcher, that the affair had been amicably settled, was able to state that the village could reckon itself once more in debt to him, and mentioned the case of a colleague at Middlesham who had recently been presented by grateful inhabitants with a bicycle. Later came information that Miss Bulwer had discharged her housemaid, with a month's wages in lieu of notice; the driver of the station fly, in the course of a chat with his fare, ascertained the cause for her dismissal was that Miss Bulwer had understood her (the housemaid) to say, before the Londoner's call, that she believed Mr. Gleeson was a bachelor, whereas the departing housemaid declared she had only mentioned that he was clean-shaven. All the same the decision of the arbitrator stood; Miss Bulwer was declared to be the owner of the right of way, but graciously permitted the inhabitants to use it.

Few of the villagers had walked along the path before the locked gate was placed there, and no one showed any anxiety to do so now that it was thrown open.

"A most satisfactory beginning," said Mr. Gleeson to his young wife. "Nothing could be more auspicious. Now, we are about to take up the task of breaking down some barriers on our own account. Your help, dear, will be specially needed."

"I haven't your tact."

"You have something better, my love," he replied gallantly. "You have charm. Together we ought to do a great work."

"The place is beautifully quiet now," she remarked.

"If there's peace to be found in the world," quoted Mr. Gleeson, "a heart that is humble may hope for it here."

"The girls are complaining."

"They will soon become accustomed to the village and its surroundings. It takes time for a Londoner to settle down. The silence," he went on, going to the window, "is to me most impressive."

"It appears to strike them as being dull."

That evening, when the two were consulting the local directory, taking down names and perfecting arrangements, a sudden uproar started near the open windows, and the servants came hurrying in to make protest against the noise; Mary and Emma urged that the master ought to go out and see what was happening. Looking through the open window the group could see that every man, every lad, every woman carried articles capable of producing clamour: some bore dustpans, some toy drums, some fire-irons. Mr. Gleeson felt able to give an explanation to the affrighted woman. It had, he believed, to do with bees; not quite certain about details, he felt sure it concerned bees swarming or something of the kind.

"I don't want to be stung," said cook nervously. "Wasps always make straight for me!"

The crowd stopped at a house facing the green, and there the hullabaloo increased to such an extent that Mr. Gleeson, finding his cap, announced an intention of putting a stop to the row without further delay. The women expected the turmoil would cease directly he reached the scene; they observed that he spoke to one or two, remonstrating with them; the folk seemed to be making an explanation, and he again used argumentative gestures; they appeared to order him to go away and, after one or two further efforts, he retired. The uproar continued.

"Not bees," he announced, entering the room. "No! My dear, just send the maids to the kitchen."

The girls went.

"A primitive custom," he explained, "with which I was not previously acquainted. It seems a retired farmer living at the house in question lost his wife three months ago."

"Surely a strange way of expressing sympathy."

"That is not exactly the idea. The retired farmer has married again married the nurse, and the village thinks it not quite right."

"It isn't right," she declared warmly. "I consider the villagers are quite justified in their action."

"I don't agree with you, dear."

"If I died," she contended, "and you married again in such a short time, I should be very much gratified in looking down to find that people—"

"Why do you say 'down'?" The contention in the Gleesons' house rivalled the demonstration in the roadway.

Mutual apologies having been made the next morning.

"I spoke without thinking of what I was saying, my love."

"I suppose, dear, I am too sensitive."

The great task came up before them to be tackled. Mr. Gleeson made a short speech to his wife on the subject, calling it a scheme for welding the village into one harmonious whole, and they were both gratified by this neat way of putting the case. One harmonious whole, echoed Mrs. Gleeson. One harmonious whole, he repeated firmly.

So the two set out, furnished with cards, to call upon residents; an undertaking the more necessary and excusable because residents had made no attempt to call upon them. They divided the task, arranging to meet two hours later and report progress of affairs, and meanwhile said farewell in an affectionate style outside the house; two little girls, looking on with a scandalised air, prepared to run off to tell their respective mothers.

"Good luck, dear," said Mrs. Gleeson.

"Bon voyage, ma cherie," he replied. They kissed again.

At the time appointed she returned with satisfaction and triumph announced on her attractive young features. Her husband had not arrived, and she strolled across to some children who were fixing wickets for a game; they drew the stumps and retired to another corner of the green.

"Shy little things," remarked Mrs. Gleeson.

She flag-signalled with a lace handkerchief to her husband, who could be seen walking slowly in the distance, but he was gazing at the dusty road in a thoughtful manner and did not respond; she ran to meet him and to take his arm.

"Well?" he asked shortly.

Everybody had said yes, she answered with enthusiasm. No sooner had she given the invitation than they accepted. The vicar, the Congregationalist minister, the auctioneer (who was also insurance agent, and local representative for Chipley's Celebrated Guanos), the schoolmaster, Crutchley, the postman, two labourers, and the man who usually stood outside the Three Bells with a wisp of straw between his teeth every one of these and others she had secured, every one had made careful note of the date.

"And you?" she asked.

Mr. Gleeson confessed his record was not so excellent. Miss Bulwer delayed him for thirty-five minutes, and, a grievance still rankling, managed in that time to intimate that she bossed the village.

"Her own phrase," he said excusingly.

Miss Bulwer flattered herself she performed the task well, and certainly did not propose to allow new-comers to interfere. Miss Bulwer agreed that the barriers of class should be broken down; she came of a Liberal stock, and her father sat in Parliament once for nearly a year, but rather than meet Crutchley or any of his set on friendly terms, she would willingly be burnt at the stake.

"But surely, dear, it was an error, if you don't mind my saying so, to tell her that we had invited anybody else."

"Thought it fairer," he replied.

"I said nothing of the kind to some of mine."

"You should have done."

"Pardon me," said Mrs. Gleeson, "but perhaps you will admit that my plan proved more successful."

"Those two sisters, the dressmakers, are coming," he went on, declining to argue the point, "and three other women accepted and promised to be with us providing nothing better turned up in the meantime. Singularly frank and open in their speech," he remarked, with a sigh. "They went so far as to ask me what we expected to make out of it."

"I like people to be genuine." "There are limits," he said, "which should not be exceeded. Let us go in and reckon up the number of guests."

The two small girls who had seen them kiss each other took up a position near the fence, watching with undisguised curiosity as Mr. and Mrs. Gleeson sat at the window completing arrangements. As these proceeded Mr. Gleeson regained something of his early enthusiasm. He intended to make a speech to the company, once the visitors were assembled, and his wife suggested that if his mind was made up in this regard, he had better rehearse; he walked up and down the room, using appropriate gestures, the while the two little spectators held on to the fence in their anxiety to miss nothing.

"Did you remember to telegraph to the Stores?" he demanded, breaking off. "I did."

"And have the things arrived?" "Not yet. But they never fail." "Find a man," he ordered, "the one outside the Three Bells, and send him off at once. Unless I see to everything, there is always a muddle!"

Full justification for the issuing of this command was found when the man returned with the case; it had duly arrived by the mid-day train and would, he reported, have remained at the station until goodness knew when if he had not been sent to fetch it. The man offered to prise open the lid, and on seeing the contents made the announcement that the two shops of the village would not be best pleased to hear that goods similar to those which might have been purchased at their establishments had been imported from town. Asked by the anxious young hostess to give his own opinion, the man said he was all for liberty and freedom, and letting people do as they liked, but he felt bound to say that home industries ought to be patronised. He had often argued this in the Three Bells, and felt he ought not to say behind people's backs anything he did not dare to speak in front of their faces.

"All the same," he added, accepting the shilling, "I shall pop round in good tune this evening. You can rely upon me. My word's as good as me bond."

Now the two maids began to fly to and fro. Now Mr. Gleeson set out chairs on the lawn at the back in preparation for an overflow meeting. Now furniture was moved and the pianoforte opened. Now one of the maids ran across to hire twenty cups and saucers, and returned from the shop with the message that only regular customers were obliged in this way; the cups and saucers could be purchased, or they could be let alone, but no third alternative existed. Mr. Gleeson went over his speech once more and, on the suggestion of his wife, introduced a more pronounced tone of geniality, leaving out some of the sterner views concerning the value of friendship. Mrs. Gleeson's sketches were set in a good position.

Mr. Gleeson tried "I am a Jolly Mariner" and decided he had found himself in worse voice. At seven o'clock they were ready for the thirty-five guests, and Mr. Gleeson snatched a few moments to practise a smile of welcome, one that would indicate gratification without degenerating into a broad grin.

"We shall find them rather difficult at first," he mentioned. "I must get you to help me, my dear, to make them feel thoroughly at home from the very outset. Wish you had thought to order some crackers."

"Sorry!"

"In Stepney, if you remember, the pulling of these and the wearing of paper caps at once put everybody at their ease. What's the time now?"

She exhibited her watch.

"Mary asked the constable just now whether anything of the kind had ever been arranged before and he said 'No'."

"Did he say anything else?" asked Mr. Gleeson.

"He added 'And never won't again, neither'."

"The ability of peering into the future," he remarked, nettled, "is a gift denied even to the village policeman. He seems to have the idea that no one can do right excepting himself."

"There's a knock."

Please, ma'am (announced Mary), Mr. Crutchley, the butcher, has sent over to know whether we want a joint for Sunday, because if so we had better say so in good time. Ask the messenger (replied Mrs. Gleeson) to tell Crutchley that we shall, only trouble him in the case of chops and steaks; the larger orders have been placed in town. Very well, ma'am. Mary, returning three minutes later, apologised for the message she had now to deliver; Crutchley sent word that where the Gleesons procured their joints there they could procure their chops and steaks; Crutchley told the messenger to add that he was not in the habit of being under an obligation to any one.

"I disliked the man," declared Mr. Gleeson warmly, "from the very first. Understand, my dear, please, that not another penny of mine is to be spent in his shop not another halfpenny."

Another ring, and Mary, with a look of greater satisfaction, announced the vicar.

"Ah," said the visitor, entering breezily, "Liberty Hall, Liberty Hall. This is extremely satisfactory. How are we this evening? Settling down to country life? That's good. Before I forget it, there are two or three funds under my control, the finances of which are in rather what shall I say?"

"Low water."

"Capital!" declared the vicar, with enthusiasm. "The very phrase! Now I'm not going to bother you, and hate above all things any suspicion of begging, but if you have your cheque-book handy How very, very kind of you! A great day, for Murford Green here's a fountain pen for Murford Green when you two delightful people decided to take up your residence here. Thank you so much: I'll blot it. Equally divided, shall we say? A thousand obligations. I have a number of letters to write; will you forgive me if I run off? Pray give my sincere regards to all the dear people. All the dear people. The dear people. Dear people. People." The voice disappeared in the manner of a ventriloquist's entertainment.

A note from the schoolmaster. The schoolmaster was sorry, but he had only just ascertained that the Rev. Mr. Barton, Congregationalist minister, had been asked, and in these circumstances the schoolmaster begged to be excused. A note from Mr. Barton. Mr. Barton, having ascertained that the schoolmaster had been invited, felt it impossible to meet that gentleman until he had withdrawn certain remarks concerning Passive Resistors, and hoped Mrs. Gleeson would permit him to defer his visit. The postman called at the back door to say that he could have spared an hour, and would have spared an hour, but talk was going on in the village, and until this received contradiction it was more than his position, as a Government official, was worth to set foot inside the house. Mary, answering her master's impatient reprimand, declared she had asked for further particulars; the postman, with a deep blush, assured her it was not a subject he could discuss with a single young woman; on Mary insisting, he referred her to a Mrs. Larch, living in one of a row of cottages not far away. The Gleesons, greatly disturbed, requested the maid to fly in that direction and obtain details. As Mary went out of the front gate they noticed the two invited labourers, dressed in black suits.

"Beg pardon, missy," they heard one of them say, "but if it ent a rude question, is there going to be any beer purvided at this affair what's to come off this evening?" The maid gave an answer and ran on.

"Not?" they echoed amazedly. "Very well then! No bloomin' beer; no bloomin' us!"

Other excuses came. The odd man of the Three Bells alone remained unaccounted for, and he arrived, pulling at the garden gate, which he should have pushed, and solving the difficulty by climbing over. Approaching the open window, he lurched across the flower-bed, took off his hat to Mr. Gleeson, blew a clumsy kiss to Mrs. Gleeson.

"Not coming in," he said, with a wink. "No fear! Not me! Got my reputation to consider. I sh'd never 'old up my 'ead again. Warm lot, you Londoners. Thank goodness I was born 'n bred in the country. Honest man, that's what I am, and I don't care who says I'm not. You never catch me 'ugging a girl in middle of the roadway. Not me!''

A council was held so soon as the maid came back. Mary had assured Mrs. Larch that her master and her mistress were married, for she herself was present at the wedding, and the lady offered two suggestions: one that Mary's eyesight was defective, the other that people only used a foreign language when they desired to say something that could not be spoken in decent English. Mary, having delivered the news, stood back and waited.

"Have you no suggestion to make, my dear?" asked the worried Mr. Gleeson. His wife shook her head despondently.

"Excuse me, sir," said the maid, with respect, "but me and Emma have been talking it over, and as she says the doctor ordered you quiet, and you haven't yet succeeded in letting the house at Kensington, what's to prevent us from—"

"Get the A.B.C.," he ordered. "We'll find out what time there's a train back to town in the morning."

XV

REWARD FOR COURAGE

The Committee gave Mr. Mayor the time to put on, with the aid of his man, the official garments. One member asked who was looking after Enderby, and the agitated young secretary ran into the largest room in the Town Hall, returned with the satisfactory assurance that the man was seated in the front row, well guarded by friends.

"These brave chaps," remarked the member who had put the alarming inquiry, "often have a peculiar strain of er, modesty in their disposition. You can never quite depend upon them as you would on ordinary people. Mr. Secretary, what's the programme for the afternoon? Have you drawn up an agenda? Don't call on me, if you can help it, but if it's absolutely necessary, of course."

Mr. Secretary exhibited the sheet of foolscap paper; members of the Committee whose names figured there expressed approval; the rest mentioned a fear that they might not be able to stay until the end.

"Mr. Mayor!"

His Worship came forward to be greeted by those acquainted with him, to be introduced to others. Everybody said it was good of the Mayor to give up so much of his time, and he declared it was good of them to do so.

"But some one," he went on, with determination, "some one must give me a sort of a notion of an idea of what I'm supposed to talk about. I want a few facts pencilled down, just to go on with, as it were." The secretary produced a type-written document, tendered a case containing a medal. "I see!" nodding as he glanced at the sheet. "Jumped in at risk of life. Brought child to bank. Persuaded with difficulty to give name and address. Very fine, indeed. Capital. First-rate. Now, how long shall I take? Thirty minutes?"

"Less than that, Mr. Mayor, if you like."

"As you please," said his Worship, rather nettled. "I'm never a believer in long speechifying. Time we made a start, isn't it? Look in, and tell them I'm coming, and they'll be ready to applaud. What's the chap's name again? Enderby. George Enderby. Right you are!"

A good audience had assembled, and several ladies, subscribers to the gift, were present. Two were talking deferentially to a puffed faced man in the front row; they scuttled off to their seats as the platform people arrived. The man inspected his boots, shifting them uneasily. Mr. Mayor rapped the table with an ebony hammer, and said, in his most genial manner, that of all the duties imposed upon him during his year of office not one had given so much pleasure as this. They were probably acquainted with the facts and he would give them briefly. George Enderby, residing at 42, William Street, by occupation a house decorator, but at present out of work, was walking near the canal on the evening of Friday, the seventeenth of June. Some children were playing near the bank, and, in the endeavour to reach a piece of wood that was floating on the water, one little girl of six years of age suddenly slipped and Mr. Mayor read the type-written sheet to the end, took off his pince-nez.

"Let George Enderby," he ordered, "be kind enough to step up on the platform."

The friends of the puffed-faced man took him by the elbows; he resisted their efforts and was heard to say that he would see everybody hanged before he made a public exhibition of himself. An awkward delay occurred; the Mayor repeated his directions. The secretary hurried down from the platform, and induced George Enderby to consider afresh his decision. He went up the steps with every sign of reluctance, and stood there, turning cap in hands.

"Enderby," said the Mayor, with an air of heavy benevolence, "kindly answer one or two questions. In what condition of mind were you when you performed this gallant act?"

"I wasn't boozed," replied the man defensively, "if that's what you're driving at. I'd had a glass or two, but I wasn't abs'lutely oiled!"

"That is not quite what I mean. What I want to find out is, were you thinking at the time of the value of human life, and how necessary it is that it should be preserved at all costs?"

"If you must know, I waddent thinking nothing of the kind. Don't worry myself about such matters."

"I see!" said the Mayor, slightly taken aback. "And forgive my curiosity but what were your sensations when you brought the child ashore? What was uppermost, so to speak, in your thoughts?"

"I was wondering whether I sh'd catch a nasty cold!"

"No, no!" said the Mayor, reproving the audience. "This worthy fellow is answering my questions to the best of his ability. Tell me, now," turning again to the man on the platform, "have you performed many gallant actions of this kind in your life before?"

"I ain't."

"Never, perhaps, had the opportunity?"

"Plenty of opportunities," retorted Enderby, "but not fool enough to take advantage of 'em!"

It was so clear he was becoming nettled that the secretary whispered to Mr. Mayor; his Worship proceeded to speak, at some length, on the subject of bravery, making allusions to the boy who stood on the burning deck, to Grace Darling, and to others. Eventually, and to the obvious relief of Enderby, he presented the purse, handed over the medal, and allowed the man to return to the front row. There Enderby and his friends made no attempt to conceal restiveness during the remainder of the speeches. The occupants of seats at the reporters' table sent a note to the young secretary, reminding him that the recipient had not acknowledged the rewards.

"No," replied Enderby, with resolution,

"I jolly well won't. Made myself quite conspicuous enough as it is, and if I tried to talk from the platform I sh'd only make myself more conspicuouser than before. I may also add it's dry work listening to all this cackle."

"Don't lose the medal."

"You take charge of it for me," he requested. "May overlook it somewhere if I take it with me now!"

It was the secretary's first essay in management of public affairs and he congratulated himself, in leaving the Town Hall, on the fact that everything had gone well; the Mayor had said at the end, "Very smooth and satisfactory!" The case with the medal bulged the inside pocket of his coat, and this would not have mattered only that he was going, later, to see a young woman whom he loved, and give to her a full report. Wherefore he stepped on a tram-car and was conveyed to William Street.

"May be back at any moment," said the neighbours. "What's to-day? Tuesday? Well, she has to be at Willesden by seven in the morning, and she usually gets home, comparatively speaking, early. Other days its quite late before she Here she is!"

Mrs. Enderby was grateful to the secretary for bringing the medal, and said so. She wished he had also brought the money that had been collected, but this, she knew, was an extravagant aspiration. Mrs. Enderby admitted it was difficult, at times, to make ends meet; thanks be, she had fair health and strength. Six children, all living, and no one could say they ever wanted for food. Yes, it did seem a pity Enderby was out of a job, but, after all (cheerfully), it made very little difference at home, because if he earnt money he spent it all himself. How long? Oh, a matter of eleven years or so. Good afternoon, sir, and thank you.

"Now, I wonder," remarked the young secretary to himself, "I wonder if they were right in putting his name on that medal!"

William Pett Ridge – A Short Biography

William Pett Ridge was born at Chartham, near Canterbury, Kent, on 22nd April 1859.

His family's resources were certainly limited. His father was a railway porter, and the young Pett Ridge, after schooling in Marden, Kent became a clerk in a railway clearing-house. The hours were long and arduous, but self-improvement was Pett Ridge's goal. After working from nine until seven o'clock he would attend evening classes at Birkbeck Literary and Scientific Institute and then to follow his passion; the ambition to write. He was heavily influenced by Dickens and several critics thought he had the capability to be his successor.
From 1891 many of his humourous sketches were published in the St James's Gazette, the Idler, Windsor Magazine and other literary periodicals of the day.

Pett Ridge published his first novel in 1895, A Clever Wife. By the advent of his fifth novel, Mord Em'ly, a mere three years later in 1898, his success was obvious. His writing was written from the perspective of those born with no privilege and relied on his great talent to find humour and sympathy in his portrayal of working class life.

Today Pett Ridge and other East End novelists including Arthur Nevinson, Arthur Morrison and Edwin Pugh are being grouped together as the Cockney Novelists.

In 1924, Pugh set out his recollections of Pett Ridge from the 1890s: "I see him most clearly, as he was in those days, through a blue haze of tobacco smoke. We used sometimes to travel together from Waterloo to Worcester Park on our way to spend a Saturday afternoon and evening with H. G. Wells. Pett Ridge does not know it, but it was through watching him fill his pipe, as he sat opposite me in a stuffy little railway compartment, that I completed my own education as a smoker... Pett Ridge had a small, dark, rather spiky moustache in those days, and thick, dark, sleek hair which is perhaps not quite so thick or dark, though hardly less sleek nowadays than it was then".

With his success, on the back of his prolific output and commercial success, Pett Ridge gave generously of both time and money to charity. In 1907 he founded the Babies Home at Hoxton. This was one of several organisations that he supported that had the welfare of children as their mission.

His circle considered Pett Ridge to be one of life's natural bachelors. In 1909 They were rather surprised therefore when he married Olga Hentschel.

As the 1920's arrived Pett Ridge added to his popularity with the movies. Four of his books were adapted into films.

Pett Ridge now found the peak of his fame had passed. Although he still managed to produce a book a year he was falling out of fashion and favour with the reading public and his popularity declined rapidly. His canon runs to over sixty novels and short-story collections as well as many pieces for magazines and periodicals.

William Pett Ridge died, on 29th September 1930, at his home, Ampthill, Willow Grove, Chislehurst, at the age of 71.

He was cremated at West Norwood on 2nd October 1930.

William Pett Ridge – A Concise Bibliography

Minor Dialogues (1895)
A Clever Wife (1895)
An Important Man and Others (1896)
Second Opportunity of Mr Staplehurst (1896)
Mord Em'ly (1898)
Outside The Radius. Stories of a London suburb (1899)
A Son of the State (1899)
A Breaker of Laws (1900)
London Only. A Set Of Common Occurrences (1901)
Lost Property (1902)
Up Side Streets – Short Stories (1903)
Erb (1903)

George And The General (1904)
Next Door Neighbours (1904)
Mrs Galer's Business (1905)
The Wickhamses (1906)
Name of Garland (1907)
Speaking Rather Seriously (1908)
Sixty Nine Birnam Road (1908)
Table d'Hôte. Tales (1910)
Splendid Brother (1910)
From Nine to Six-Thirty (1910)
Light Refreshment (1911)
Thanks to Sanderson (1911)
Love at Paddington (1912)
Devoted Sparkes (1912)
The Remington Sentence (1913)
Mixed Grill (1913)
The Happy Recruit (1914)
The Kennedy People (1915)
Book Here – Short Stories (1915)
Stray Thoughts from W. Pett Ridge (1916)
Madam Prince (1916)
The Amazing Years (1917)
Special Performance (1918)
Well To Do Arthur (1920)
Just Open. Short Stories (1920)
Richard Triumphant (1922)
Lunch Basket – Tales (1923)
Miss Mannering (1923)
Rare Luck (1924)
Leaps And Bounds (1924)
A Story Teller – Forty Years In London (1923)
Just Like Aunt Bertha (1925)
I Like To Remember (1925)
Our Mr Willis (1926)
London Types Taken From Life (1926)
Easy Distances (1927)
The Two Mackenzies (1928)
The Slippery Ladder (1929)
Eldest Miss Collingwood (1930)
Led by Westmacott (1931)

William Pett Ridge also wrote a play titled "Four small plays".

www.ingramcontent.com/pod-product-compliance
Lightning Source LLC
Chambersburg PA
CBHW021934170626
46807CB00007B/3100